For more than forty years,
Yearling has been the leading name
in classic and award-winning literature
for young readers.

Yearling books feature children's
favorite authors and characters,
providing dynamic stories of adventure,
humor, history, mystery, and fantasy.

Trust Yearling paperbacks to entertain,
inspire, and promote the love of reading
in all children.

Pieces of Gax

Written and illustrated by

Mark Crilley

A YEARLING BOOK

Visit us on the Web! www.randomhouse.com/kids

Educators and librarians, for a variety of teaching tools, visit us at www.randomhouse.com/teachers

The Library of Congress has cataloged the hardcover edition of this work as follows:
Crilley, Mark.
Akiko : pieces of Gax / Mark Crilley.
p. cm.
Summary: Sixth-grader Akiko and her friends from the planet Smoo travel to the upside-down
city of Gollarondo, where an accident befalls Gax the robot and a search begins for all
his missing pieces.
ISBN: 978-0-385-73044-0 (trade) — ISBN: 978-0-385-90430-8 (glb)
[1. Life on other planets—Fiction. 2. Robots—Fiction. 3. Japanese Americans—Fiction.
4. Adventure and adventurers—Fiction. 5. Science Fiction.] I. Title.
PZ7.C869275Ab 2006
[Fic]—dc22
2006006033
ISBN: 978-0-440-41895-5 (pbk.)
Reprinted by arrangement with Delacorte Press

Printed in the United States of America

August 2008

10 9 8 7 6 5 4 3 2 1

First Yearling Edition

Random House Children's Books supports the First Amendment and celebrates the right to read.

This book is dedicated to
my dear friend Ian Jackson,
and to his wife, Francesca,
and sons, Thomas and George.

*"Roommates for six months,
Roomies for a lifetime."*

Chapter 1

My name is Akiko. You know how whenever something really amazing happens to you, you just can't wait to tell all your friends about it? And how sometimes the amazing thing that happened to you is so incredible and mind-blowing that even after you've told your friends about it they think you made the whole thing up? And how sometimes you don't even *dare* to tell any of your friends about the amazing thing that happened to you because it all took place while you were on another planet in a distant galaxy, surrounded by aliens and robots and exploding volcanoes and stuff, and if you were foolhardy enough to even *begin* to tell your friends a *word* of it, they would decide then and there that you were completely and irreversibly out of your mind?

Don't you hate that?

Well, hey, right now I don't care whether people who read this think I'm making it up. If they think I'm a few cards short of a full deck, they can go right ahead and think that. My only concern is to put all this stuff down on paper, in the exact order it happened, and to get the details right. Because if I don't write it down and I end up forgetting some of it after a while, that really *will* make me crazy.

Here's what you need to know:

1. I'm an ordinary sixth grader. A human being, I swear.
2. A few years back I became friends with a bunch of space people from a planet called Smoo.
3. Since then, every few months or so, these friends of mine come to Earth and say they

need to take me into outer space because . . . well, they've always got one excuse or another, and it always sounds pretty reasonable at the time.

All right. Now I can tell the story.

When it comes to meeting up with me on Earth, my friends from Smoo have made some pretty weird entrances over the years: appearing in rocket ships disguised as police cars, intergalactic transit systems on shopping mall rooftops, you name it. But the way they showed up this last time really raised the bar in terms of sheer ridiculousness.

I was on vacation with my mom and dad. We were staying at my aunt Lucille's house in Minnesota. (Aunt Lucille, who has an unexplainable fondness for big floppy hats and bright orange lipstick, has made some pretty weird entrances of her own over the years, but that's a different story.) We'd been there for a couple of days, and my cousin Earl had grabbed his fishing poles and taken me down to Wacahoota Creek to see if we could catch anything "big enough to stick in the bathtub and scare the bejeezies outta Mom." Me, I wasn't sure I wanted to see Aunt Lucille any more freaked out than she already was on a day-to-day basis. But hey, it was my third day in the backwoods of Minnesota, and my entertainment options—even my reasons for staying awake—were severely limited.

So there I was with Cousin Earl, sitting at the end of a mossy makeshift dock with a fishing pole in my hands, staring down into the brown-black waters of Wacahoota Creek. In spite of Earl's claim that this spot was "world famous" as the best fishing hole in Putnam County, we'd caught nothing but dead leaves and, in what was possibly the low point of the vacation so far, a pair of discarded diapers from somewhere upstream.

"That reminds me of a funny story," Earl said, tossing the diapers as far as he could back upstream (thereby all but guaranteeing that we would catch them again a few minutes later). "This one's a real gut buster."

He went to his tackle box and began noisily rummaging through it. "You know what a gut buster is, right?" Earl had an amazing ability to tell "funny stories" that weren't funny and—this takes talent—really weren't even stories. They started at point A, moved on to point G, and then just sort of petered out somewhere in the middle of an entirely different alphabet.

Without waiting for me to either confirm or deny that I knew what a gut buster was, Earl launched into his diaper-related tale. I stopped listening by around the third rambling sentence.

Then, to my shock, I actually felt something tugging on my line.

"Hey, Earl . . . ," I said, then nearly bit my tongue off trying to stop myself midsentence. There, about six inches below the surface of Wacahoota Creek, was a small glass dome, the kind you would see at the top of a deep-sea submersible on the Discovery

Channel. Through the dome, which was attached to a submarine-like vessel, I saw the face of none other than Spuckler Boach, grinning from ear to ear and giving me an enthusiastic thumbs-up. Behind Spuckler, squeezing in to make sure I'd see him, was a cheerful but panicky-looking Mr. Beeba.

I blinked in disbelief: my friends from Smoo had somehow found their way into the best fishing hole in Putnam County and were inches from rising to the surface and scaring the bejeezies out of my cousin Earl.

I motioned furiously to Spuckler and Mr. Beeba to stay underwater.

"What's up?" said Earl, still rummaging through his tackle box. "Getting crawdad nibbles again?"

"No!" I said a little too loudly, setting my fishing pole on the edge of the dock. "I mean, um . . ." I tried desperately to come up with a good reason for having said "Hey, Earl" two seconds earlier, one that wouldn't encourage him to come back over. The interstellar submarine had not broken the surface of

Wacahoota Creek, but if Earl joined me on my side of the dock, he'd see it as plainly as I did. "Could, could, could you go back and repeat that last part of the story? It was, uh, so funny I gotta hear it again."

Earl turned his face in my direction, so pleased with my sudden appreciation of his genius for story-telling that he failed to notice I'd broken into a sweat. "Which part? The part about the bald-headed squirrel or the part about the surfer dude from Saskatoon?" I briefly marveled at the fact that these two topics had not only nothing to do with each other but also nothing whatsoever to do with diapers. "Um, both. You should be a stand-up come-dian, Earl, I swear."

Earl chuckled, cleaning his glasses with the hem of his T-shirt. "You are not the first person to say that."

The second Earl turned back to his tackle box, I began motioning to Spuckler that he should steer their submarine as far as he could downstream and that I would catch up with them in—I pointed to an imaginary wristwatch and splayed all my fingers two times—twenty minutes.

Spuckler drew his eyebrows together and gave me a supremely confident *gotcha-cap'n-over-and-out* nod before leaning down to pull a lever.

GLOOSHHhhhhhh

The submarine dome bubbled forth from Wacahoota Creek, sending a spray of muddy water in all directions.

"What the—" Earl whipped around and began charging toward my side of the dock.

"An octopus!" I shouted before realizing it was the worst explanation I could possibly have concocted. Earl was just a couple of footsteps from catching sight of Spuckler's sub. I bailed on talking my way out of the situation and instead jumped up and tackled Earl like a linebacker.

My plan—to the extent that I had any plan at all—was to send him flying backward across the dock toward the shore. Instead, I knocked him clear off the dock and into Wacahoota Creek. I watched with horror (and, okay, a certain amount of pleasure) as Earl flew headlong into the shallow end of the fishing hole. Then I spun around to see Spuckler's red and blue submarine rise all the way out of the water and hover there for several seconds. The upper half of Spuckler's head was visible through the dome, and he was clearly wrestling with the controls of the vehicle, trying to get it to do his bidding.

I turned back to Earl and watched him emerge from the creek, his dripping wet hair half concealed by a soggy diaper, which he was now wearing like a hat. "The heck you do that for?" he grumbled as he chucked the diaper into the mud and began fishing around for his glasses, without which, I then gratefully recalled, he could hardly see his hand before his face. If he'd still been wearing them, he'd have seen Spuckler's submarine floating in the air right behind me.

"Sorry, Earl," I said. "I was, uh, trying to stop you from knocking the bait off the dock." I rolled

my eyes at my own pathetic excuse, then listened with amazement as Earl proceeded to take it quite seriously.

"The worms, eh?" Through the shallow water I could just make out the shape of Earl's glasses, a good ten feet away from where he was searching for them. "Well, that's understandable. Those suckers cost me five bucks." No way. He was practically *thanking* me. "So didja make the save or not?"

"Oh yeah," I said, watching as Spuckler's anti-gravity submarine rose another thirty or forty feet. "All worms are, uh, present and accounted for." The caster on my rod and reel whizzed as the hook at the end of my line—still securely fastened to the exterior of the sub—rose higher and higher into the sky. Finally I just let go of the fishing pole and allowed it to be carried away like a strange anchor.

The sub turned and silently hovered directly over me and Earl, blocking out the sun for a moment and drizzling a considerable amount of creek water on both of us as it continued on its skyward path.

"What is it, raining?" Earl asked, squinting up at what must have looked to him like an incredibly thick and low-lying thundercloud.

"D-darnedest thing" was all I could manage to say as Spuckler's sub disappeared over a nearby oak tree. It was the first time in my life (and the last, I sincerely hope) that I have ever used the word *darnedest*.

Now that I felt sure that Earl's bejeezies would

remain safely intact, I rolled up my pant legs, jumped into the water, and fished his glasses from the creek. "Found your specs, Earl," I said as I trotted up to the tackle box and grabbed a dry cloth. "Here, I'll clean them off for you."

"Thanks, cuz," said Earl. Now he really *was* thanking me.

Moments later Earl had squeezed as much water out of his jeans as he could and was heading back to the house—a good ten-minute walk—to change his clothes. "Now, I don't know what you saw there in the creek, cuz," he said before sloshing his way up the dirt road that had brought us here, "but you can take my word for it: it wasn't no octopus."

"You can say *that* again," I whispered to myself, then went off into the woods in search of a certain space-faring submarine.

Chapter 2

It took me all of sixty seconds to find Spuckler's ship: red and blue rocket ships tend to stand out in the backwoods of Minnesota. It was parked in a grassy clearing, its single door propped open on one side, grayish green steam rising from its tail fins. Spuckler and Mr. Beeba stood before the ship and were gesturing frantically at me with their whole bodies, as if I needed to pick them from a crowd of other extraterrestrials equally interested in meeting up with me that day.

" 'Kiko!" shouted Spuckler. "Gitcher little Earthian bee-hind over here and gimme a hug!" He was grinning like crazy and had already bounded halfway across the clearing to facilitate my bee-hind's progress in the endeavor.

"Do accept my apologies for the gro*tesque*ly crude manner of our arrival on the scene, my dear child," said Mr. Beeba, trotting along the path cleared by Spuckler. "I *told* Spuckler that the notion of our emerging from the watery depths whilst you were in the midst of an angling expedition was as outlandish as it was fraught with perils, but did he listen to me? No."

"Lookitcha, lookitcha!" Spuckler completed the last few leaps that brought him to my side, threw his arms around me, and whirled me around three or four times before plunking my feet back on the ground. "Ever' time I see ya you're taller an' prettier. Smarter, too, I'll bet," he added with a wink.

"Smart enough to know," said Mr. Beeba, panting heavily as he caught up with Spuckler, "that one doesn't arrange a secret rendezvous by hiding one's spaceship underwater, then making one's presence known at the most inopportune moment imaginable."

"Oh yeah?" said Spuckler, poking a finger into Mr. Beeba's chest. "Well, that must mean she's smart enough to know that *one* oughta keep *one*'s trap shut if *one* doesn't want *one*'s head smacked so hard he has to spend *one* hundred and *one* days in the hospital!"

At this point I had to step in and introduce a healthier amount of breathing room between them.

"All right, all right," I said. "How about if someone tells me what's going on before my cousin Earl comes back and sees what a bunch of intergalactic kooks I've been hanging around with for the past few years?"

"Oh, you're gonna like this, 'Kiko," said Spuckler, the spat with Mr. Beeba already forgotten. "We're takin' you to Gollarondo. Yeah, that's right: Gaw-law-rondo!"

"An architectural wonder of the first order, Akiko," Mr. Beeba added. "You'll not want to miss it, I assure you."

"Now, slow down a minute," I said, knowing from experience that when Spuckler and Mr. Beeba said they were taking me somewhere, the "somewhere" tended to be in a different galaxy, and the "taking" generally resulted in my (a) being chased by aliens, (b) dodging meteors, (c) getting covered in goo, or (d) being subjected to none of the above, but something a whole lot worse. "First, before there's any talk of my going anywhere other than back to that dock, I need the two of you to promise me something."

"You name it, 'Kiko," said Spuckler, and Mr. Beeba nodded his agreement.

"No slime, grime, mud, or misery."

"Gotcha," said Spuckler.

"No being sent on missions that have virtually no hope whatsoever of success."

"Understood," said Mr. Beeba.

"No near-death experiences."

"Does that include being-knocked-near-*unconscious* experiences?" asked Spuckler before receiving a very sharp elbow to the gut, courtesy of Mr. Beeba.

"You have my word, Akiko," said Mr. Beeba, "that the visit to Gollarondo will be a vacation unlike any you have ever had, and that includes a distinct absence of misery, missions, and near-death experiences."

"Oh, come off it, 'Kiko," said Spuckler. "You know ya wanna go, and the choice couldn't be plainer. Come with us, ya got guaranteed thrills 'n' spills. Stay here, ya got Cousin Earl an' a bucket fulla worms." Spuckler gave me a knowing look while lazily reeling in an imaginary fish with an imaginary fishing pole. "Now, which one're ya gonna choose?"

Spuckler had called my bluff. Was it really that obvious that I wanted to go with them, regardless of the risks that might come with the bargain? Judging from the grin on Spuckler's stubbly face, it was *more* than that obvious.

One peek over at the spaceship decided it once and for all. There, just inside the doorway of the ship, were Gax and Poog. Gax had his robotic head cocked eagerly to one side, while Poog, floating in the shadows, simply blinked and smiled.

How could I say no to these guys?

"Okay, okay," I said, happily caving in. "So where's my replacement robot?"

"Perfect!" said Mr. Beeba, dancing a jig back to the spaceship. "You'll not regret this, Akiko. I promise!"

Moments later we had made the necessary adjustment to the Akiko-replacement robot—the modest tan I'd acquired in recent days was replicated on her at the touch of a button—and sent her back to the dock with my fishing pole (once we'd gotten it unhooked from the spaceship, that is).

As I watched my robotic twin disappear into the foliage of backwoods Minnesota, I marveled at the fact that Cousin Earl would return to an entirely different Akiko from the one he'd left and yet remain blissfully unaware that anything had changed.

"Better get a move on, 'Kiko," bellowed Spuckler from the ship. "We got six star systems t' get through before the day is out. Seven, if you count this here dinky one that you're a part of."

I climbed aboard and quickly found my seat in the surprisingly roomy vehicle.

"IT IS A PLEASURE TO SEE YOU AGAIN, MA'AM," said Gax, his tin-can voice containing more emotion than usual. "I FEARED THAT AFTER OUR LAST ADVENTURE YOU'D GIVE UP ON SPACE TRAVEL."

"What, and miss the chance to hang with my

favorite robot in the whole universe?" I said, reaching over to pat Gax's helmet. "Not on your life."

Gax rocked contentedly from side to side.

A series of garbled syllables filled the ship as Poog floated over to greet me.

Mr. Beeba listened carefully, then provided his translation: "Poog says he will do everything in his power to see that no harm befalls you during this excursion. And as you know, Poog doesn't make promises lightly." Poog smiled at me and moved close enough that I could see my reflection in his big shiny eyes.

"Thanks, Poog," I said, giving him a gentle hug. "You're the best."

Poog gurgled a pleased response that was soon drowned out by a loud hum from the engine. "Hold on tight, 'Kiko," hollered Spuckler from the driver's seat. "Next stop: Gollarondo!"

Chapter 3

"So just what exactly *is* Gollarondo," I asked, peering out one of the windows as Earth receded into the stars, "and why is it such a big deal?"

"Gollarondo is a city on the planet Smoo," replied Mr. Beeba, his eyes gleaming, "and there are a great many things that make it a *'big deal.'* "

He did a couple of highly exaggerated air quotes with his fingers to make it clear that *big deal* was *my* choice of words, not his.

"Firstly, it boasts mag*nif*icent examples of glipto-hoobian architecture, all of them im*pec*-cably restored and preserved. Secondly, it is known throughout the universe as a center of gracious living, academic excellence, and unparalleled mastery of the culinary arts. 'All who live in Gollarondo,' goes the saying, 'are well bred, well read, and well fed.' Finally—and this is my personal favorite feature—it is home to the SMATDA: the Smoovian Museum of Ancient Tomes and Dusty Artifacts. I promise you an *extensive* tour, conducted by yours truly."

Mr. Beeba closed his eyes and inhaled deeply. In his mind, I imagined, he was already strolling happily through the corridors of the SMATDA, holding forth on every object he saw whether we wanted him to or not.

"Oh yes, and it's upside down," he added.

"I see," I said, before realizing that I didn't see at all. "Hold on. What's upside down?" I asked.

"Gollarondo," Mr. Beeba said. "Now, don't worry about the admission fees for the SMATDA, Akiko. I've bought each of us three-day passes, and—"

"Wait, wait, wait," I said. "You're telling me that Gollarondo is a city." I looked Mr. Beeba in the eye, trying to make sure he was saying what I thought he was saying. "A city that's upside down."

"Quite," said Mr. Beeba. "Now, here is the SMATDA catalog," he continued, pulling out a gray tome as thick as a telephone book and depositing it in my lap. "I suggest you give it a thorough going-over and make a list of the exhibits you most want to—"

"Wait. No. Stop," I said, waving my fingers in front of Mr. Beeba's mouth as if trying to snap him out of a spell. "How can a city—an *entire city*—be upside down?" Before he could answer, I added: "And don't say anything about the SMATDA."

Mr. Beeba frowned, rolled his eyes, and let out a disappointed sigh. "Look, Akiko, you'll see for yourself when we get there. Suffice it to say that Gollarondo is upside down. Just as some cities are right side up." He shrugged, as if to indicate that building cities upside down was a matter of personal preference, and that it was in very poor taste to make too much of a fuss about it. "It's really quite simple."

Sensing that I'd get little more from Mr. Beeba on the subject, I decided to let it go for the time being. "Right. Well, I guess I'd better have a look at this catalog, then."

"Dive on in, my dear child," said Mr. Beeba, his face brightening. "It begins with a section on ancient tomes, but I'll hold you *entire*ly blameless if you opt to skip right on to the section on dusty artifacts. It's every bit as engrossing as it sounds."

A few hours later we arrived in the upper stratosphere of Smoo: the starry sky outside the windows turned indigo, then purple, then a cool blue. Spuckler steered the ship into a sharp descent, causing my stomach to leap up into my throat for a terrifying second or two. "Best way to get to Gollarondo is by shootin' in over the Moonguzzit Sea," he explained. "You just sit tight, 'Kiko. I'll have us there b'fore ya know it."

Sure enough, it was only a matter of a few minutes—and a few miles of cruising perilously close to the blue-green waters of the Moonguzzit

Sea—before Gax announced that our final destination was in sight. "IF YOU KEEP YOUR GAZE FOCUSED IN THIS DIRECTION," he said, pointing with a spindly mechanical arm, "YOU SHOULD BE ABLE TO SEE GOLLARONDO JUST UNDER THE TOP OF THOSE CLIFFS AHEAD."

"Thanks, Gax," I said. "But I'm pretty sure you mean just *over* the top of the cliffs."

Gax gave me a quizzical stare.

"Or just *on* the top of the cliffs."

Gax continued staring.

"How about *near*?"

"I AM PROGRAMMED FOR THE HIGHEST DEGREE OF VERBAL ACCURACY POSSIBLE, MA'AM," he said.

"I'm sure you are, Gax, but—"

"Thar she blows, 'Kiko," Spuckler called from the front of the ship. "Dead ahead!"

All at once I understood what both Mr. Beeba and Gax had said about Gollarondo. Yes, it was upside-down. And yes, it was *under* the cliffs.

The entire city had been built on the underside

of a cliff face jutting out over the Moonguzzit Sea.
All the buildings—gleaming white facades and red-
tiled roofs—had been painstakingly built in reverse:
their foundations laid in the stony surface above,
their spires pointing down to the waters below.
Nearly every building was connected to another
building by some sort of walkway. And as we drew
nearer, I saw that the people of Gollarondo, in spite
of having built their city upside down, were no better adapted to living in it than I was. Indeed, the *in-
teriors* of the buildings were all right side up: I

saw people through the windows as we glided into town, going about their business—shuffling papers, watering plants—as if living and working inside an upside-down city were the most natural thing in the world.

"It's . . ." I searched for a worthy adjective but could find nothing but the most obvious one. ". . . upside down."

"Yes, Akiko," said Mr. Beeba. "I thought I'd already mentioned that. Now, there's the SMATDA over there, just behind the hanging gardens. Don't get too excited just yet, though. It doesn't open until tomorrow morning."

Spuckler steered our ship between a pair of massive upside-down towers, zooming up and over a walkway connecting them. I pressed my face against the glass portal nearest me, trying to get a good look at a couple of men strolling—right side up—across the walkway.

"Love this place," said Spuckler. "*Weird*. But I love it."

"They . . . ," I began, still struggling to find something intelligent to say about what I was seeing. "They built the city upside down. The whole city. Upside down."

"Yes, well . . . ," replied Mr. Beeba with a chuckle, "it wouldn't have made much sense to build *half* the city upside down, now, would it?" He continued chuckling, as if the idea of building cities upside down was supremely logical as long as you were consistent about it.

Spuckler pulled the spaceship onto a platform—

a sort of upside-down train station—and parked it beside a number of other ships. Looking up, I saw benches and potted plants above me, all attached to the cobblestone ceiling as if it were a floor.

"This is the . . . strangest place I've ever seen," I said.

"You sure?" asked Spuckler. "You've seen some pretty weird stuff in your time, 'Kiko."

I thought for a moment of all the places I'd seen since first visiting Smoo a couple of years earlier: the Sprubly Islands, the planet Quilk, the Jaws of McVluddapuck.

"Okay," I said. "But in the top three, for sure."

Chapter 4

We all got out of the ship and I immediately stepped over to a guardrail at the edge of the platform. Leaning on it and looking over, I got a vertigo-inducing view of the Moonguzzit Sea hundreds of feet below, its tiny waves crashing noiselessly against the shore. Looking straight across from me, I saw a spectacularly inverted city skyline: Spanish colonial rooftops, ornate gilded spires, and even gently swaying palm trees, all entirely upside down.

A high-pitched warble erupted near my left ear and I turned to find Poog at my side, a gentle expression on his pale purple face.

"Poog says to be cautious when leaning on

guardrails in Gollarondo," Mr. Beeba explained. "Some of them are quite old and have been known—on rare occasions—to give way."

I immediately jumped back, removing my weight from the seemingly sturdy guardrail. The drop from Gollarondo to the Moonguzzit Sea did not look survivable.

"Thanks, Poog," I said, and Poog smiled.

"All right, enough standing around," said Spuckler. "Let's get some chow. I'm so hungry I could eat a hunnerd Smud Burgers and still have room for dessert."

"I'm afraid he's not exaggerating, Akiko," said Mr. Beeba. "Come. I know a lovely little café not too far from here."

Mr. Beeba led us away from the platform and across a walkway into the center of the city. As we went along, I took in all the details of the incredible cityscape surrounding us: a window washer working his way down to the roof of a building, then climbing back up to the ground floor; birds flying—right side up, of course—from one upside-down tree to another; children trying to retrieve a kite that had gotten snagged in a garden gate far above their heads.

"... and once we've all finished breakfast," said Mr. Beeba, whose description of the next day's schedule I'd been tuning in and out as we went along, "we'll head over to the SMATDA and begin the first of the dozen-odd tours I've planned. Any questions?"

"I've got a question," I said.

"Please," said Mr. Beeba.

"Why would anyone in his right mind build a city upside down?"

The blood drained from Mr. Beeba's face. He jumped in front of me and slapped one of his big white-gloved fingers across my lips.

"Shhhh!" He looked over each shoulder, snapped back to lock his eyes on mine, and remained silent as a group of laborers strode past us on the walkway. Once they were safely out of earshot, Mr. Beeba resumed speaking, this time in an urgent whisper. "Akiko, you must never ... *never* ... ask that question in Gollarondo."

"But—"

"Shh!"

Mr. Beeba leaned his head to one side and fairly shouted "Good morning!" at a woman passing with a baby carriage. His smile was entirely unconvincing, though I could see all his teeth and a good portion of his gums. "Lovely day, is it not?"

The woman gave Mr. Beeba an odd look and increased her speed as she passed.

Mr. Beeba waited until the walkway cleared, then continued. "The citizens of Gollarondo are ex-*tremely* touchy about people referring to their city as"—he leaned forward and made his voice so quiet it required lipreading—"upside down."

"But it *is* upsi—"

"Hssh!" Mr. Beeba's eyes were the size of ostrich eggs.

A group of students entered the walkway, slowing to stare at Mr. Beeba as they passed. "Run along!" Mr. Beeba barked at them. "You'll be late for class!"

I waited until the walkway cleared again, then whispered: "All right, so why did they build this city . . ." I spent several seconds searching for a good synonym for *upside down* before realizing there was none. ". . . the way they built it?"

Mr. Beeba paused, took a breath, and said: "I haven't the faintest idea." He gave a little shrug and added: "How could I? No one ever talks about it."

My mouth hung open for such a long time that Mr. Beeba lifted a hand and closed it for me.

I looked from Spuckler to Mr. Beeba to Gax to Poog. None of them looked even slightly troubled by the fact that an entire city had been built upside down and no one knew why.

"Akiko," Mr. Beeba said gently. "The truth of the matter is that the people of Gollarondo feel that their city is right side up. That it is, in fact, the *only* city in the universe that is right side up. To a Gollarondoan, it is you and I who live in upside-down cities."

"But that's"—I let out a sigh of exasperation—"crazy."

"Maybe it is, and maybe it isn't." Mr. Beeba wobbled his head a bit, refusing to take sides in the matter. "But rather than expending your energies on deciding who is crazy and who isn't, I would encourage you to enjoy Gollarondo for what it is: one of the loveliest cities you've ever seen, regardless of what direction its rooftops point in." He waved a hand toward Gollarondo's inverted skyline, inviting me to look at it with a fresh perspective.

There was no denying it. Gollarondo *was* one of

the most beautiful cities I'd ever seen. In fact, its upside-down-ness was a big part of what made it so beautiful. And though I still thought the Gollarondoans were a bit nutty, I did find myself wishing I could live in their city for a while just to see what it was like.

"Can we eat?" said Spuckler.

Chapter 5

Mr. Beeba's favorite café, Chez Zoof, was located in the oldest section of the city. The walls were decorated with yellowed photos of intergalactic personalities—some humanoid, some decidedly not—who had dined there over the years. We opted to eat outside on the balcony, where the rusting cast-iron guardrails stretched across a spectacular view of Gollarondo's upside-down skyline.

While we waited for our food, Mr. Beeba swiftly steered the conversation back to his favorite subject. ". . . and so I did what any conscientious citizen would do when coming across a SMATDA employee chewing gum whilst installing an exhibition: I told him of his misdeeds and alerted the authorities immediately." He looked at us as if he expected us to break into spontaneous applause. "That lad was fired the very next day, or so I'm told." Still no applause. "Yes, well, I'm not to be blamed if you can't appreciate a good story, rivetingly told."

"Where's the grub?" asked Spuckler, loudly enough for any and all waiters in town to hear. "All's I ordered was three dozen Bropka sausages, extra spicy, with blurgle cheese and all the toppings, plus a side order of moolo rings and an ice-cold jug of smagberry cider. What's takin' 'em so ding-dang-diddly long?"

"Patience, Spuckler," said Mr. Beeba. "I'm sure they're not accustomed to having a single customer order enough provisions to feed a small army."

Just then the waiter arrived with food. To Spuckler's unbridled fury, it turned out to be a large egg perched atop a plateful of noodles: the dish Mr. Beeba had ordered.

"Have a look at this, Akiko," said Mr. Beeba. "I told you that the people of Gollarondo are highly skilled in the culinary arts. Well, here we have one of their masterpieces: a jeelee egg."

I leaned over and inspected the egg, catching a tantalizing whiff of the noodles as I did. It was about five inches from top to bottom, with a glossy black shell. "What's so special about it?" I said.

"The exterior is an actual eggshell, but the *interior* is entirely prepared by hand from the finest ingredients available. No one knows the secret of how they get the food into the egg without breaking the shell." Mr. Beeba let me ponder this for a moment, then added: "Jeelee eggs are available only here in Gollarondo, and even then they're hard to come by. Indeed, this is the last one in town at the moment, according to the waiter."

"So what does it taste like?"

I shot a glance at Spuckler, who was eyeing the egg enviously.

"Ab. So. Lutely. Scrumptious." Mr. Beeba's eyes rolled back in his head as he reveled in the glories he was about to experience. "I assure you it is quite unlike any dish you have ever tasted."

Spuckler's stomach growled noisily. *Roared* might be a better way of putting it, actually.

"Why, it is a meal unto itself," continued Mr. Beeba, "and holds within it flavors so rich and delectable that the merest *men*tion of the word *jeelee* sets people's mouths watering."

Spuckler's tongue moved slowly back and forth across his upper lip.

"Actually, Mr. Beeba," I said, "maybe it's not such a good idea to describe that egg in too much detail right now."

"Oh, but Akiko, a verbal appreciation is essential to enjoying the jeelee egg properly." Mr. Beeba placed his fingers gingerly around the egg and lifted it from its bed of noodles. "The interior of the egg is a creamy gravy—not too salty, not too sweet—in which are suspended morsels of meat so tender and juicy, so expertly marinated that they quite literally melt in your mou—"

"Gimme that thing!" Spuckler snatched the egg out of Mr. Beeba's hand, grabbed a spoon, and prepared to unleash its ingredients with a single crack.

"Spuckler!" Mr. Beeba leaped out of his seat and bolted toward Spuckler. "Return that egg to me at once!"

I felt my chair jerk to the side as Mr. Beeba's foot hooked one of its legs. In an instant he took to the air and flew straight into Spuckler's lap, sending both of them tumbling onto the balcony with a thunderous crash.

The jeelee egg, miraculously unscathed, rolled out of Spuckler's hand and twirled across the balcony toward the widely spaced struts of the guardrail. There was nothing to stop it from rolling off the edge of the balcony and plunging all the way down to the Moonguzzit Sea.

Well, nothing but *me,* anyway.

I rocketed from my chair, took three huge strides, and dived after the jeelee egg like a baseball player sliding for home plate. Skidding across the tiled surface, I watched—almost in slow motion—as my fingers closed around the egg at the last possible moment, halting its fall even after it had teetered over the balcony's edge.

I lay there panting for a moment, staring with relief at the egg in my hands, mildly amazed at what I had managed to do.

"Well *done,* Akiko!" said Mr. Beeba, extricating his limbs from Spuckler's and rising to his feet. "Most impressive!"

"Hot diggity dog biscuits, 'Kiko!" said Spuckler. "I ain't never seen moves like that in all my days."

"YES, MA'AM," said Gax, who was nearest to me. "YOUR REFLEXES HAVE GREATLY IMPROVED SINCE YOU FIRST CAME TO SMOO."

"Thanks, guys," I said as I rose to my knees and inspected the jeelee egg for cracks. "Looks like it's still in good shape."

"Now, Spuckler, if you can manage to *control* yourself," said Mr. Beeba, pausing to clear his throat, "perhaps we can all enjoy the contents of the jeelee egg together."

"Hey, I can't be held responsible for my actions on an empty stomach."

I chuckled and grabbed hold of the guardrail as I stood up.

ggggrrrraaaaAAAAAAK!

All at once the rusty iron guardrail gave way.

"Yyaaaahhh!"

I teetered over the edge of the balcony and caught a terrifying glimpse of the Moonguzzit Sea, hundreds and hundreds of feet below, before pinwheeling my arms, tossing the jeelee egg into the air, and utterly losing my battle with gravity.

My world turned to a blur as I tumbled over, thrust my hands toward what I hoped was the edge of the balcony—it was, thank goodness—and held on for dear life.

"DON'T LET GO, MA'AM!" Gax said, racing across

the balcony as fast as his wheels would carry him. "I'LL GET YOU!"

I pulled myself up high enough to get one elbow onto the edge of the balcony. Then I saw it: the jeelee egg, smashed to bits, its contents forming a wide, shimmering circle of gravy just inches away from my face, and Gax, hurling himself forward at top speed, heading straight toward its remains.

"No, Gax!" I shouted. "Don't—"

ssssslllluuuuuuuurrrrrrrshhhh

I watched helplessly as Gax's wheels slid into the gravy, reversing direction after it was already impossible to gain traction, his robotic eyes dilating as he realized the mistake he'd made.

sssssssssssssssssss

"Nooooo!" I cried.

But it was already too late.

Gax shot right past me, sliding neatly between my nose and what was left of the guardrail nearby.

"Noooooooooo!" I shouted again, powerless to stop what was transpiring before my eyes.

Craning my neck as far back as I could, I watched Gax silently tumble down to the Moonguzzit Sea, gravy shooting off his wheels in all directions, his rotating body blindingly white against the turquoise waters.

I opened my mouth, but no words came.

Spuckler, Mr. Beeba, and Poog reached the edge of the balcony just in time to see Gax's body grow smaller . . .

. . . and smaller . . .

. . . and smaller . . .

. . . before finally hitting the water, creating a tiny dot of white in the sea a good half mile from the shore.

No words were spoken as Mr. Beeba and Spuckler hoisted me onto the balcony. Silently, they poked their heads back out to gaze at the spot where Gax had vanished. You could almost hear the cogs turning in everyone's heads as the reality of what had just happened began to sink in.

Gax is gone. I knew it, but I couldn't bring myself to say it out loud. *He's . . . gone!*

Just then the waiter emerged from the interior of Chez Zoof, carrying a tray piled high with food.

"Where's the bottomless pit that ordered all these sausages?"

Spuckler didn't even turn his head. He just kept staring down into the waters of the Moonguzzit Sea.

"I ain't hungry anymore."

Chapter 6

Mr. Beeba hurriedly paid the bill and off we went, speeding back to the spaceship.

As we dashed from one walkway to another, weaving through crowds of disapproving Gollarondoans, Poog flew over to Spuckler's left shoulder and unleashed a brief torrent of warbly syllables.

"Quite right, Poog," Mr. Beeba said between hoarse gasps of air. "I'm sure Gax's buoyancy canisters will function quite adequately."

"That ain't what I'm worried about, Poog," said Spuckler, his pace quickening with each stride. "Gax sinkin' is the least of our problems right now."

Mr. Beeba considered Spuckler's words for a

moment. Then his eyes widened and his cheeks lost most of their color. Poog's face displayed a similar reaction: shock, followed by mild panic.

"Now, now, now . . . ," Mr. Beeba said, "don't assume the worst. If we can get to him before Hoffelhiff does, all will be well."

"That's a big *if,* Beebs," said Spuckler. "Hoffelhiff'll have a head start on us. A *long* head start!"

"Hoffelhiff?" I asked as we sprinted into a shadowy tunnel in the middle of a towering upside-down cathedral.

"Nugg von Hoffelhiff," explained Mr. Beeba, his words echoing crazily off the tunnel walls. "He rules the seas beneath Gollarondo. There is a long-standing agreement whereby anything and everything that falls from Gollarondo"—he raised a finger, signaling that he would need several seconds of violent wheezing before finishing the sentence—"belongs to Hoffelhiff in perpetuity."

"No way!" I said. "You mean this guy's gonna be able to keep Gax for, for . . ."

". . . *ever*," said Mr. Beeba, his face now twisted into a grimace of despair.

"Not if *I* have anything to say about it!" growled Spuckler. "That 'bot belongs to me, an' I ain't lettin' no two-bit thievin' weasel steal 'im!"

Soon we arrived back at the ship and piled in as quickly as we could. By the time I strapped myself into my seat, Spuckler had already revved the engine. Seconds later we blasted into the skies of Gollarondo, narrowly missing walls, rooftops, and several wildly flapping clotheslines as Spuckler spun the ship into a nosedive.

ffffffvvvvvvvvvvvvvv

A low-pitched hum filled the ship as we began to pick up speed.

"Now, Spuckler," said Mr. Beeba, "d-d-don't do anything rash. A high-speed entrance into Hoffelhiff's territory could be interpreted as a declaration of hostile intentions."

"My intentions *are* hostile," said Spuckler, "an' gettin' hostiler by the minute!"

vvvvvvvvvvvvvvVVVVVVVV

The hum grew steadily louder and higher.

I leaned forward and peered through the windshield at the surface of the Moonguzzit Sea, which was drawing near at an alarming rate. "Spuckler, um . . ." I tried to think of a delicate way of putting it. "Remember what happened *last* time you did stunt piloting over the Moonguzzit Sea?"

"Don't worry, 'Kiko," said Spuckler, punching buttons on the dashboard. "We ain't gonna be *over* the Moonguzzit Sea."

Spuckler kept the ship on a near-vertical path of descent, showing no sign at all of changing course.

VVVVVVVVVVVVV

Poog issued a loud gurgly warning, which Mr. Beeba translated as: "If you hit the water at this speed, you could cause severe damage to the navigation system!"

"*I'm* the only navigation system we need right now," bellowed Spuckler, bracing himself for impact. Mr. Beeba and I did likewise.

VVVVVVVVVVVVVVV

The blue-green surface of the Moonguzzit Sea

was now less than a hundred feet below us. It whirled and rushed toward the windshield in a matter of seconds. I closed my eyes just before—

vvvvvVVVVVVVVVVVVVV

FOOOOOOOOOOOOOOOOOSSSSSSSSHHHHH!

The sound of the ship hitting the water was like a bomb going off. I was thrown forward from my seat, and the restraining belts dug deep into my stomach and shoulders.

When I opened my eyes, the interior of the ship was bathed in an undulating green glow. Outside the ship's portals I saw nothing but water and silvery bubbles racing past. We were moving much more slowly now but had nevertheless already reached a point far below the water's surface.

I had no reason to be surprised by the submarine capabilities of Spuckler's ship—I'd seen them in use back at Wacahoota Creek, after all. Still, experiencing the move from air to water as a passenger was a different matter entirely.

"Awright, Gax," said Spuckler, activating an

octagonal radar screen above his head. "Gimme a sign. That's all I need."

toong . . . . *toong* . . . . *toong* . . . .

A quiet note sounded while a single green dot pulsated on the radar screen.

"Yes!" Spuckler turned the steering wheel three full rotations to the left. "You just stay put, li'l buddy," he added, his voice hopeful for the first time since Gax had fallen off the balcony.

"We won't letcha down."

Chapter 7

Soon we were moving through the water at full speed.

toong. . . . toong. . . . toong. . . .

The note began to repeat more frequently, the green dot on the radar screen pulsing in time with it.

"Be cautious, now, Spuckler," warned Mr. Beeba. "Hoffelhiff's men may well be in the vicinity."

"You can betcher fuzzy little *head* hairs they're in the vissimity," said Spuckler, and for once Mr. Beeba opted not to correct him. "With all the time it took us t' get down here, Hoffy's thugs could have Gax right where they want 'im by now."

I swallowed and cleared my throat. "Are, uh, Hoffy's thugs armed and dangerous?"

"They better hope they are, 'Kiko," said Spuckler. " 'Cause *I* sure am."

Poog floated over to the dashboard and uttered several hushed syllables.

"Poog begs to differ," said Mr. Beeba. "You may well be dangerous—you generally are—but at present you are not the least bit armed."

Spuckler shot Poog an annoyed glance. "He don't know what he's talkin' about. See these suckers over here?" Spuckler pointed at a bank of red buttons to his right. "You're lookin' at three of the most advanced pieces of submersible aqua-techtronic weaponry in the galaxy. Number one: kloxurian torpedoes. Number two: laser-guided phortane missiles. Number three: wog-flurk rockets. *Twenny* of 'em."

Poog floated over to the dashboard for a brief examination. He then issued a prolonged warbly assessment.

"Oh dear" was all Mr. Beeba could bring himself to say.

"What?" said Spuckler, turning his head to confront both Poog and Mr. Beeba. *"What?"*

"Kloxurian torpedoes?" said Mr. Beeba. "Lethal, but only to us: the launch door is jammed."

Spuckler turned angrily to the bank of red buttons. "Hmf. Coulda *sworn* I fixed that last year." He gripped the steering wheel and made a show of indifference. "Yeah, okay, but we still got two outta thr—"

"Laser-guided phortane missiles?" said Mr. Beeba. "Most effective. *If* you had not left them at home in your living room."

Spuckler turned again to the bank of buttons. After a very long pause he said: "Dining room."

"As for the wog-flurk rockets," Mr. Beeba said with a sigh, "Poog says that there is no such thing and that you probably made them up simply to impress us."

"Awright, that is *enough* outta you," said Spuckler,

stabbing an angry finger in Poog's direction. "Why don't you just keep your trap shut and . . . and . . . be *mysterious* for a while!"

toong . . . toong . . . toong . . . toong . . . toong

The light on the radar was now blinking at a furious pace.

"Awright, Gax," said Spuckler, switching on a pair of bright yellow headlights in the nose of the ship, "show yourself, already."

I peered into the blue-green depths outside the windshield. There were bubbles, bits of seaweed, and schools of three-eyed alien fish, but no sign of Gax.

Then I saw him: a glint of white straight ahead.

"Good goin', Gax!" Spuckler shouted. "Ya did it! Ya gave 'em the slip!"

Gax was floating thirty feet or so below the surface, bobbing gently up and down and waving at us with a mechanical arm. As we drew nearer, Spuckler focused the headlights squarely on him and guided the ship forward until we were right next to him.

"Incredible!" I said. "It looks like he didn't even get a scratch."

"Ain't nothin' 'credible 'bout that," said Spuckler, offended on Gax's behalf. "Gax units are th' toughest little 'bots in the universe. And Gax is tougher'n any of 'em."

By now Spuckler had maneuvered some sort of communications tube through the water and hooked it up to Gax's head.

"That was some mighty fine divin', Gax," said Spuckler into an intercom dangling from the ceiling. "Whatcha doin'? Trainin' for the 'Bot Olympics?"

"THANK YOU FOR ARRIVING WITH SUCH SPEED, SIR," came Gax's tinny voice from a speaker on the dashboard. "SHALL I ATTACH MYSELF TO THE SHIP'S HULL?"

"Hop to it, little guy," said Spuckler. "We ain't got all day."

"I don't like this," said Mr. Beeba. "Where are Hoffelhiff's sentries? They should have gotten here before us."

"Beebs, sometimes ya jus' get lucky," said Spuckler. "Try t' enjoy it, 'stead of bein' such a party pooper."

Chapter 8

TUNK. GLENK. P'CHANK!

Metallic noises echoed through the ship as Gax attached himself to it from the outside.

"He's on, he's on, he's on," said Spuckler, his voice buzzing with excess energy. "Awright, buckaroo bambinos, let's hightail it on outta here!"

Spuckler banged a few buttons on the dashboard with his fist. The ship shuddered, groaned, and began rising. I peeked out the windows for any sign of Hoffelhiff's men but saw nothing. We were making a clean getaway. It seemed Spuckler was right: sometimes you just get lucky.

When we reached the surface, Spuckler pulled a

lever and the whole top third of the ship peeled back like the roof of a convertible, one section sliding under another, until we had a clear view of the sky, the sea, and Gollarondo above. A fishy, seaside smell filled my nostrils, and a strong breeze tossed my pigtails up against my cheeks. There, attached to the front of the ship by four suction-cup-tipped legs, was Gax, looking none the worse for his recent fall.

"Gax!" I cried with relief. "Are you okay?"

"I'M QUITE ALL RIGHT, MA'AM," replied Gax, bouncing happily as he inched his way up to the top of the ship, "APART FROM HAVING TAKEN ON A BIT OF UNNEEDED BALLAST." A spout emerged on one side of his body and . . .

ffffsssssssssshhhhhhhh

. . . the water that had seeped into Gax during his undersea tour came spritzing out. Then a door popped open on the opposite side of his body and . . .

sssshhhhhhlupp!

. . . a good-sized fish was forcibly ejected. It

flipped several times through the air before splashing into the sea.

Spuckler laughed, loud and long. It was partly
because of the ejected fish, but mostly, I suspect,
it was an expression of the relief he felt at having
his longtime robotic sidekick back within arm's
reach.

"C'mon, Gax," said Spuckler, grabbing Gax with
both hands and hoisting him into the interior of the
ship. "Now, next time you wanna pull a stunt like
that, do me a favor and use a bungee cord or somethin', will ya?"

A high-pitched bleating noise blasted my ears as
Poog made a sudden, urgent announcement.

"Spuckler," said Mr. Beeba before Poog had even
finished, "Hoffelhiff's men have spotted us. They'll
be here any second. We've got to go. *Now!*"

"Done," said Spuckler, yanking a knob near the
steering wheel. "Hold on tight, ever'body. We . . .
are . . . *gone!*"

BRRRRRRRUUUUUUUMMMMM

The stench of spent fuel filled the air as the engine roared to life. The whole ship rocked and vibrated from stem to stern and back again. Spuckler punched several buttons on the dashboard and we all braced ourselves for a swift and sudden liftoff.

RRRRMMMM-KUK-RRRRMMMM-KUK-KUK

The engine's roar, having built to a crescendo, was now interrupted by unpleasant knocking sounds. Then, more disturbingly, the roar itself began to die down to something more along the lines of a loud hum.

RRRRRRRrrrrmmm-KUK-KUK-KUK-rrrmmm

"Spuckler!" shouted Mr. Beeba, his eyes buggy with fear. "Get this ill-equipped bucket of bolts out of the water immediately! Hoffelhiff's men are almost upon us!"

"I'm tryin', ya idgit, I'm *tryin',*" shouted Spuckler, hammering wildly at buttons I'll bet had nothing to do with the engine at all.

rrrrrmmmmmmmmmmmmmmm

My heart sank as the engine began to die altogether.

Then:

P'KUK!

P'CHAAAAaaaaaaaaaaaawwwwwwwwww

Within seconds the only sounds were the wind, a few seabirds in the distance, and the waves of the Moonguzzit Sea gently lapping against the hull of the ship.

Spuckler pounded his fist on the dashboard and muttered a long sentence that included the phrases *rag-nattered hootly-tootin'* and *expired warranty.*

FOOOOOOSSSSSHHhhhh

Water on the left side of the ship churned and sprayed as a steel gray vehicle emerged and rotated until its nose—decked out in compact but deadly-looking artillery—was pointed straight at us. It was as big as our ship. Maybe bigger.

"A fogglenaut," said Mr. Beeba, his voice cracking with anxiety. "Hoffelhiff's most feared sentries.

A single one of them can s-sink a ship ten times our size."

FOOOOOOSSSSHHH

FOOOOOOOSSSSSHHHH

Two more fogglenauts emerged on the opposite side of our ship; then . . .

FOOSH- FOOSH- FOOSH-FOOSH

More and more of them surfaced, each filling a spot unused by the others, until finally there were

66

sixteen in all, encircling us as neatly as numbers on a clock face.

KUNK KUNK KUNK

Our ship rocked back and forth as I felt something attaching itself to the underside of the hull. The fogglenauts all backed up a bit, enlarging their circle until it was the size of a baseball diamond. Something big—really big—was beneath our ship, and about to surface.

fffffOOOOOOOOOSSSSHHHhhhh

Mr. Beeba, Poog, Gax, Spuckler, and I all looked on helplessly as our ship was carried up and out of the water. We were now on the deck of what looked to be some sort of submersible aircraft carrier. Water poured off our ship and flowed across the deck into gigantic drains on all sides.

"Good heavens," said Mr. Beeba, the only one of us who dared make an assessment of the situation. "We're . . ."

He swallowed and shook his head.

". . . doomed."

Chapter 9

Soon we were sailing across the Moonguzzit Sea (or rather, flying just above its surface, since the vessel beneath us doubled as a high-speed hovercraft) on our way to a nearby island where Hoffelhiff lived.

"Don't nobody worry," said Spuckler, sounding more than slightly worried himself. "I know a fella who cut a deal with Hoffelhiff once. Said he was a pretty reasonable guy, actually."

Mr. Beeba snorted, as if the very idea were preposterous. "*Reasonable* is not the word that comes to mind when I think of Nugg von Hoffelhiff."

"Why, is he really mean or something?" I asked.

"Not exactly, Akiko," said Mr. Beeba. "Hoffelhiff

is a renowned eccentric. His oddball behavior has made him a favorite topic of discussion among psychiatrists, psychologists, and podiatrists." (I was pretty sure a podiatrist was a foot doctor, but I decided not to call Mr. Beeba on it.)

"Don'tcha fret none, 'Kiko," said Spuckler. "Jus' leave the talkin' to me, an' we'll be back in Gollarondo b'fore ya know it."

In a few minutes Hoffelhiff's island came into view. It was little more than a huge rectangular rock jutting out of the sea, with a few pockets of greenery spread across its upper surface. In the center of the island was Hoffelhiff's fortress, a vast structure that changed architectural styles every few hundred feet. It looked as if the architect who'd designed it had kept changing his mind about what kind of place he wanted to build. "See what I mean, Akiko?" said Mr. Beeba. "Even his home is off its rocker."

We were jetted into a cavernous opening in the side of the island, large enough to accommodate the hovercraft and all the fogglenauts with plenty of room to spare. Ten of Hoffelhiff's men then escorted us from the ship, all of them toting a variety of weapons, decked out in body armor, and grinning at us like fishermen who'd just hauled in their best catch of the year.

They took us to a craggy stone wall into which two passageways had been cut. The passage on the left was brightly lit and led upward, presumably connecting with Hoffelhiff's fortress. The one on the right led downward, toward . . . well, it was really anyone's guess at this stage. The fact that it was damp, dingy, and devoid of lighting wasn't very encouraging, though.

Two of the men lifted Gax onto their shoulders and carried him toward the door on the left.

"Now, just a goldurned minute!" cried Spuckler as he attempted to halt them, only to find that *he* was being halted by the four men nearest him. They grabbed him first by his arms, then by his legs and torso and even his neck as he continued to struggle against them.

It was too late. Gax was gone: the two men carried him into the corridor on the left and up around a corner, and disappeared.

"Ya can't separate us!" Spuckler bellowed. "We're a team! We stick *together,* dagnabbit!"

One of Hoffelhiff's men—a tall, thin man with dark glasses who I assumed was the leader of the crew—leaned over and spoke to Spuckler with the calmness of a dog trainer addressing a disobedient Chihuahua. "That robot is the property of Nugg von Hoffelhiff. You four, on the other hand, are thieves and will be dealt with accordingly."

I couldn't believe my ears. "Th-thieves? I'm sorry, mister, but you've made some kind of mistake here."

The dark-glasses guy turned to me with a patient smile. "First of all, the name is Flamstaff, not mister. And second of all, I don't make mistakes. We caught you attempting to abscond with the robot. The robot belongs to Master von Hoffelhiff. Therefore"— he waved a hand, inviting me to dispute the facts in the case—"you are thieves."

I gasped and sputtered a bit but could find nothing to say in response.

"He's quite right, actually," said Mr. Beeba, more concerned with being on the proper side of the argument than anything else. "There's no disproving the logic of his conclusion. Top-notch reasoning, any way you look at it."

Spuckler and I glared at Mr. Beeba. Had he utterly lost his mind?

"Airtight, really," he added, as if it would help matters.

Spuckler exploded in a fit of rage: "Will you shut your ding-danged doodly-hoodly—" One of the men slapped a hand over Spuckler's mouth, reducing his verbal attack on Mr. Beeba to a very long and very muffled growl.

"Enough," said Flamstaff. "Within a few hours you will have the opportunity to defend yourself before a judge in Master von Hoffelhiff's court. If he upholds your claim on the robot in question, it will be returned to you." I shot a glance at Spuckler. This news succeeded in calming him down quite a bit, though I could see he didn't entirely believe it. "Until then, I am putting all of you to work in the sorting room."

I turned to Mr. Beeba and whispered to him: "The sorting room? What's that?"

"I have an idea, Akiko," he replied, "but let's wait until we get there to see if I'm right."

Mr. Beeba, Poog, and I followed as Spuckler was carried into the passage on the right. Before long we arrived in a vast room with powerful lamps hanging from the ceiling. In the center of the room were huge stone tables piled high with old clothing, household items, and all sorts of other junk. It looked like a flea market that had been hit by a miniature tornado. Lined up on one side of the room were ten trolleys, each bearing a large wicker basket. On each basket hung a sign. The signs read:

HATS

GLOVES & SCARVES

OTHER ITEMS OF CLOTHING

COINS

JEWELRY

EYEGLASSES

CHILDREN'S TOYS

BOOKS & PERIODICALS

TOUPEES

ALL OTHER ITEMS

"A sorting room," said Mr. Beeba. "But of course. He'd need one, wouldn't he?"

"All right," said one of the guards. "Get to work. And don't put anything in the wrong basket. Master von Hoffelhiff gets *very* angry when that happens." He dragged a knobby finger across his throat to emphasize the point.

The guard joined the others at the entrance to the room, where they began playing some sort of dice game, one that had presumably been interrupted by our sudden arrival at the fortress.

Having no choice but to follow the orders of our well-armed captors, Spuckler, Mr. Beeba, Poog, and

I went to one of the tables and began trying to make sense of which items belonged in which basket.

"Where did they *get* all this stuff?" I asked, surveying the piles on the tables.

Spuckler grumbled his reply: "Same place they got Gax from: Gollarondo."

"It's quite natural if you think about it, Akiko," Mr. Beeba explained. "Things are falling from Gollarondo all the time. Headwear, it would seem, more than anything else." I followed Mr. Beeba's gaze to the basket marked HATS. It was piled high with every kind of hat imaginable.

"Picture yourself out for a stroll in Gollarondo," said Mr. Beeba. "Your hat gets blown off by a strong gust of wind. Whereas in most cities you could just chase after it, in Gollarondo nine times out of ten— *fwoop!*—it sails clear down to the Moonguzzit Sea." He thought for a moment, then added: "Sort of makes you wish you were a hatmaker in Gollarondo, doesn't it? No shortage of business for *them,* I should think."

"Wow." I was impressed. "Hoffelhiff could make a fortune just reselling the stuff that comes falling down to him every day."

"Could?" said Mr. Beeba. "He *does*, Akiko. And has been doing so for many, many years. Come on, then," he added. "We've got some sorting to do."

And so we all began the task of sorting Nugg von Hoffelhiff's windblown loot. I soon saw that it was a never-ending occupation, since every time we began to make a dent in one of the piles, a chute would

open in the ceiling and deposit yet another heap of stuff.

As the hours went by, I had nothing to do but think about the mess we'd gotten into. Or rather, the mess *I'd* gotten us into.

"I'm sorry, guys," I said to Spuckler, Mr. Beeba, and Poog as I tried in vain to separate a scarf from a pair of spectacles. "This is all my fault."

Spuckler, who had until this moment worn a look of intense frustration and anger, turned to me with his eyebrows drawn together in concern. "Now, that ain't true, 'Kiko," he said. "You ain't got no business talkin' that way. Or even *thinkin'* that way."

"Absolutely," said Mr. Beeba, who interrupted his search for a matching sandal to address me directly. "In circumstances like this, one should never assign blame to an individual." He thought for a moment, then added: "With the possible exception of Spuckler, of course."

Spuckler smacked Mr. Beeba soundly on the side

of the head (eliciting raucous laughter from the guards), then turned back to me with the sweetness of a choirboy. "What happened today wasn't nobody's fault. It happened all on its own, and now we ain't got no choice but to jus' deal with it."

"But it *is* my fault," I said. "If I hadn't leaned against that guardrail—"

"Stop right there, Akiko," said Mr. Beeba. "*If I hadn't* is one of the most profoundly dangerous phrases in the English language. If I were you, I'd never again venture into a sentence that begins with those words. They lead to sorrow, and often to madness."

"But I'm only telling the truth."

"*But I'm only* is another bad one." Mr. Beeba's mouth was beginning to curve up at the corners. "Best stay away from those sentences as well."

I smiled in spite of myself.

"How about sentences that begin with *how about*?"

Mr. Beeba smiled and made an exaggerated show

of considering the idea. "Oh, I suppose they're harmless enough," he said, "though I'm much more fond of sentences that begin with *generally speaking, ipso facto,* and *to a large degree.*"

I laughed and rolled my eyes. "You are such a goofball."

Chapter 10

Our sorting chores carried on late into the night. Not that we could *tell* it was night: it was a windowless room, and we had to keep track of time based on periodic announcements from Poog. Finally, around three in the morning, things stopped coming through the chutes in the ceiling, and we were able to completely clear the tables of the accumulated stuff in a matter of an hour or two. Just as Spuckler was depositing the last article—a ratty old toupee that I shuddered to think anyone would actually *buy*—in the proper basket, Flamstaff burst into the room and announced that our trial would begin shortly.

"This way, quickly, quickly," he said as he steered us toward a corridor leading up and away from the sorting room. "The judge invariably rules against those who are late for their own trials."

Soon we arrived in a large oak-paneled room with a raised platform on the far end, an empty jury box to the right of the platform, and very little else. In the middle of the platform was a tall straight-backed chair. Next to it was a small table with a basket on it. The basket was filled to overflowing with what looked to be monster-sized walnuts. "Bognuts," explained Mr. Beeba. "Hoffelhiff's favorite snack."

"All rise!" shouted Flamstaff, in spite of the fact that no one in the room was seated. "His Honor the Esteemed and Honorable Judge Hoffelhiff is honorably honoring us with his presence!"

"Judge Hoffelhiff?" I said. "What's going on here? Is the judge related to Nugg von Hoffelhiff?"

"We should be so lucky," said Mr. Beeba. "In all likelihood the judge *is* Nugg von Hoffelhiff." He paused and added with a surprising degree of sympathy: "It's a *very* small island. Doubling up of duties is unavoidable, really."

From behind a curtain on the platform stepped a short, heavyset man dressed in robes and a powdered wig. His face was pink and pockmarked, his nose as big and round as a mandarin orange. He stomped over to the chair, sat down, and immediately began cracking the bognuts with his teeth.

One or two minutes (and several bognuts) later, Hoffelhiff leaned forward and trained his eyes on Spuckler, Mr. Beeba, Poog, and me, as if noticing us for the first time.

"Who are these people?" he said. "What are they doing here?"

Flamstaff answered: "They are charged with attempted burglary, Your Honor. We caught them red-handed as they tried to take a robot from waters belonging to Master Hoffelhiff."

"Me, you mean."

"Yes, Your Honor."

"That's not burglary," said Hoffelhiff as he munched on a bognut. "There's no building."

Flamstaff cleared his throat. "I beg your pardon, Your Hon—"

"Burglary's when you break into a building and make off with something." He swallowed noisily. "Nothing to do with fishing something out of the water."

Mr. Beeba grinned and whispered to me: "Things are going well."

"Be that as it may," said Flamstaff, "they are also charged with banditry."

"What, they took the robot at gunpoint?"

Flamstaff seemed thoroughly baffled. "Gunpoint?"

"Or a knife to the throat," said Hoffelhiff before cracking open another nut. "Banditry's armed robbery. Can't be a bandit if you don't have a weapon."

"Yes, well, they, uh"—Flamstaff scratched his head—"weren't technically armed at the time."

Mr. Beeba chuckled giddily. "Things are going *very* well. The charges are dropping like flies."

"You had no business charging them with burglary and banditry," said Hoffelhiff. "Simple thievery would have done the job."

"Where's my robot?" said Spuckler.

"Order in the court!" shouted Flamstaff, though Spuckler had barely even raised his voice.

Hoffelhiff yawned loudly and said: "Now hurry up and charge them with thievery before I run out of bognuts."

"Oh, come on," I whispered to Mr. Beeba. "They can't change the charges right in the middle of the trial."

"But of course they can, Akiko. We Smoovians pride ourselves on the flexibility of our legal system."

"I hereby charge you with thievery," said Flamstaff.

"And trespassing," said Hoffelhiff. "That'll stick."

"And trespassing," said Flamstaff, pausing to allow Hoffelhiff an opportunity to come up with further charges. Hoffelhiff cracked a bognut shell and thoughtfully chewed its contents before waving Flamstaff onward.

"Do you have anything to say in your defense?" asked Flamstaff.

"Yeah," said Spuckler before Mr. Beeba could stop him. "That robot is mine: *M-Y-N, mine!* You know it, I know it, and you know it too." Spuckler pointed at Hoffelhiff, himself, and—for reasons I can't explain—Poog. "Now, if you know what's good for ya, you'll give it back to me, before someone—I'm not sayin' who, but he's in this here room right now—ends up with dislocated shoulders and"—he raised and shook a threatening fist—"a great big shiner to match."

Hoffelhiff sat back and gave Spuckler's words a surprising degree of serious consideration.

"A *pitiful* defense," he said after a moment. "Not a leg to stand on. Someone else have a go."

Mr. Beeba cleared his throat, only to have Hoffelhiff cut him off. "Not you." He dug through his basket, trying to find an unopened bognut among the accumulated shells. "I don't like the way you look." Mr. Beeba, oddly enough, nodded in agreement. "Let's hear from the one with the pigtails."

"M-me?" I asked.

"Yes, say something in your defense. I'm sure you can do better than that bit about the dislocated shoulders." Spuckler squinted angrily but stayed quiet.

"Um, look," I said, trying to remember the way lawyers talked in movies and TV shows I'd seen (and feeling fairly certain that they didn't say things like "Um, look"). "There are a number of, uh, facts in this case that are, uhm, not under dispute."

"*In* dispute," whispered Mr. Beeba.

"Or even *in* dispute," I added, "if you want to put it that way." I stepped forward and began pacing back and forth, thinking it might make me look a bit more lawyerly. Hoffelhiff leaned forward with great interest.

"A robot by the name of Gax fell from Gollarondo into the Moonguzzit Sea yesterday afternoon," I continued. "A robot belonging to Mr. Spuckler Boach. Now, my client," I said, not entirely sure if Spuckler really was my client (or even what the word really meant, to be perfectly honest), "is an upright citizen who has never, ever stolen anything in his entire life."

"Providin' ya don't count that herd of Bropka lizards on the planet Thnib," said Spuckler, apparently thinking he was helping the case. "But that was a long time ago," he added, bobbing his head. "*Long* time ago."

I coughed and gave Spuckler a look that I hoped would convey *Please, in the name of all that's holy, don't say anything else.* "Judge—er, I mean . . . Master Hoffelhiff now claims possession of Gax. And there is a certain, uh, validity to this claim."

Hoffelhiff munched a bognut, smiled, and said to himself, "Things are going well."

"And yet," I said, raising a finger and feeling a surge of confidence, "I propose that a robot is different from a hat"—I ticked the items off on my fingers—"or a pair of glasses, or, or, or . . ." My confidence faltered a bit, as I was unable to think of another item but somehow felt it crucial that my list include at least three things. ". . . or, or, or a freshly baked pie accidentally knocked off a windowsill."

Hoffelhiff gazed at the ceiling as he considered this last item. "Haven't had one of those for *years*. But I see what you're driving at." He waved me onward.

I took a deep breath and decided to wrap up my case as quickly as possible.

"A robot is a *companion*," I said. "More like a family member than an article of clothing. You can't separate a robot from his owner. You just can't."

Hoffelhiff raised his eyebrows and nodded sagely.

I folded my arms in front of my chest and struck a defiant pose. It may not have been the most brilliant argument, but it was the best I could do.

"I rest my case."

Chapter 11

"The court will adjourn," said Flamstaff in an unnecessarily loud voice, "until His Honor the Honorable Hoffelhiff reaches a verdict." Mr. Beeba, Poog, Spuckler, and I began to move toward the door but were halted by Flamstaff. "Where do you think you're going?"

Mr. Beeba was the first to venture a reply: "But you said the court will adjourn."

"Yes, but that doesn't mean you can leave."

"That's precisely what it means," said Mr. Beeba.

"No, no, no," said Flamstaff. "It couldn't possibly mean that."

"It most definitely does," said Mr. Beeba, "when

employed by anyone other than yourself." He paused, then recited from memory: " 'Adjourn: to move from one place to another.' It's the second or third definition in most dictionaries."

"Which dictionaries?"

"*My* dictionaries."

"You need to get new dictionaries."

"I do not."

"You do too."

"*Do not!*"

"*Do too!*"

"I've reached my verdict," bellowed Hoffelhiff, halting the argument with a well-aimed bognut shell fired straight between Mr. Beeba's and Flamstaff's noses.

We all turned to Nugg von Hoffelhiff, who had risen from his chair and was tapping his foot impatiently. For a good half minute the room was extremely quiet, and all I could hear was the tap-tap-tapping of Hoffelhiff's foot and the inhaling and exhaling of Mr. Beeba, who was gasping so loudly I thought he might hyperventilate.

"Guilty," said Hoffelhiff.

"Things are going ... very badly indeed," whimpered Mr. Beeba, who was now on the verge of fainting.

"His Honor the Honorable Hoffelhiff has honored us with a verdict," announced Flamstaff, beaming with satisfaction. "You are guilty, all of you."

"Not them," said Hoffelhiff. "You."

"Me?" said Flamstaff. "But I'm not even on *trial*!"

"Silence!" Nugg von Hoffelhiff stepped down from the platform. "You told me the robot was ownerless and had been floating there for weeks."

Flamstaff opened his mouth several times but failed to find words. "Weeks, minutes," he said at last, "I fail to see what difference it makes."

"Makes a *world* of difference," said Hoffelhiff. "You heard what the pigtailed one said: a robot's not like a hat, or a pie. It's a *companion*."

Spuckler stepped forward excitedly. "All right, all right, so cut to the chase: do I get Gax back or not?"

"The robot is yours, good fellow," said Hoffelhiff. "Come. I'll take you to him at once."

Flamstaff was outraged. "But—"

"Another word out of you, Flammy," said Hoffel-hiff with a sharply pointed finger, "and I'll sentence you to hard labor in the bognut groves."

Flamstaff clamped his lips shut and directed his attention to the patch of floor near his feet.

"Now come along," Hoffelhiff said to the rest of us, "before I change my mind."

Nugg von Hoffelhiff led us out of the courtroom and up through a stairwell into a large hall with tall stained-glass windows. "My apologies for having detained you," he said to me, now coming across as a very kind—if somewhat scatterbrained—gentleman. "A very finely argued case, I must say," he continued. "So where was it you studied law, then?"

"Oh, you know," I said, fairly certain that he wouldn't be impressed by my mentioning Middleton Elementary, "a little here, a little there."

Finally we arrived at a small storage room in the back of the fortress. In it were a great many robots, most of them rusting and covered with cobwebs.

"No one even came looking for these poor chaps," said Hoffelhiff, blowing on one and producing a massive cloud of dust. "Your dedication is admirable."

He went up on tiptoe to pull a small wooden box down from a shelf in the back of the room. "Here's your robot, then. I'm sure you'll find him in good working order." Hoffelhiff handed the box to Spuckler.

Spuckler looked at the box. It was roughly one foot square: hardly big enough to hold a couple of Gax's wheels, much less the bulk of his body. "What is this, some kinda joke?"

"Open it; he's in there," said Hoffelhiff. "I put him there myself just an hour ago."

Mr. Beeba, Poog, and I huddled around Spuckler as he opened the carton. Inside was a metallic box with two robotic eyes on one side. The eyes immediately darted back and forth, producing a quiet mechanical hum with each move. It took me a couple of seconds to realize we were looking at Gax's head.

"Good heavens," whispered Mr. Beeba.

"What . . . in . . . tarnation?" said Spuckler, lifting Gax's head out of the box and cradling it in his hands. "Gax, li'l buddy. What've they *done* to ya?"

"Oh, right, almost forgot," said Hoffelhiff, rummaging through a nearby crate of spare parts. "You'll be wanting this, I'm sure." He handed Mr. Beeba Gax's helmet. "Didn't quite fit in the box," he added, by way of explanation.

"Ya . . ." Spuckler was in shock. "Ya took him apart." His eyes moved between Gax's face and Hoffelhiff's. "Ya broke him into pieces."

"Yes, well, I had to maximize my profits, didn't I?" said Nugg von Hoffelhiff. "The spare parts of Gax units are quite valuable these days."

Spuckler slowly turned toward me and placed Gax's head in my hands. "Hold this for a minute, 'Kiko." Then, in a fraction of a second . . .

"I'll pulverize ya!" Spuckler had Hoffelhiff by his collar and was shaking him so hard I thought he might break the man's neck. *"I'll wipe the floor with ya!"*

"Spuckler!" I cried. "You're going to hurt him!"

"This ain't hurtin' him, 'Kiko," growled Spuckler, shaking Hoffelhiff even harder. "Believe me, I'm just warmin' up!"

"Stop!" I said, setting Gax's head on a nearby crate and grabbing one of Spuckler's arms.

"Spuckler, unhand him!" shouted Mr. Beeba, grabbing the other.

We both pulled on Spuckler's arms as hard as we could, but nothing could break his grip on Hoffel-hiff's collar. "He ripped up Gax!" Spuckler cried, his eyes wild with anger. "He tore him limb from limb!"

Poog blurted something warbly and shrill, which Mr. Beeba translated as follows: "Spuckler, you fool!" (The "you fool" part was probably not in Poog's original sentence.) "This fellow may well be the only one who knows where the rest of Gax is!"

"Qu-qu-quite," Hoffelhiff managed to say while his head rocked wildly from side to side.

"He's a murderer!" Spuckler had pretty much lost it by this point. "A cannibalizer!"

"Stop, you lunatic!" shouted Mr. Beeba, leaping onto Spuckler's back, grabbing tufts of his hair with both fists and yanking with all his might. "Stop this madness at once!"

Then, suddenly:

"PLEASE, SIR." A very familiar robotic voice filled the room, freezing Spuckler like a statue. "TIME IS OF THE ESSENCE."

We all turned toward Gax's head, which sat motionless where I'd left it.

"THE REST OF ME IS NO LONGER ON THIS ISLAND, SIR," Gax's head continued. "YOU MUST LEAVE AT ONCE IF THERE IS TO BE ANY HOPE OF PUTTING ME BACK TOGETHER."

Spuckler let go of Hoffelhiff, allowing him to drop noisily to the floor. Mr. Beeba let go of Spuckler's hair and slipped down off his back. I released Spuckler's arm and crept over to Gax's side, where Poog was already hovering, listening intently.

Spuckler leaned down until his eyes were directly across from Gax's. "No longer on the island?"

"MASTER HOFFELHIFF SOLD THE PIECES OF MY BODY TO THREE DIFFERENT BUYERS YESTERDAY EVENING," Gax explained. "THE NECK TO ONE, THE BODY TO ANOTHER, AND THE WHEELS TO A THIRD. I

OVERHEARD THE ENTIRE EXCHANGE." Gax paused, then added: "ALL THREE BUYERS HAVE SINCE RETURNED TO THEIR RESPECTIVE PLACES OF RESIDENCE."

"He *sold* ya?" Spuckler's eyes were wide with disbelief. "He broke ya up and sold ya piece by piece?"

"I entirely understand your anger," said Hoffelhiff, who was by now on his feet and giving himself a thorough dusting off. "I will gladly pay you a percentage of the sale." He raised a hand, as if to stop us from thanking him. "Twenty percent. Extremely generous, by any standard."

"BEFORE YOU BEGIN THROTTLING MASTER HOFFELHIFF AGAIN, SIR," said Gax, who knew Spuckler better than any of us, "MIGHT I SUGGEST PURSUING MY NECK FIRST? IT'S IN A SMALL VILLAGE ON THE COAST. WITH AN EARLY START YOU MAY WELL RETRIEVE IT BEFORE DAYLIGHT."

Spuckler relaxed his hands, which had indeed already been curled into throttling mode, and nodded at Gax's request. "All right, Mr. 'Bot Buster," he said, turning to Nugg von Hoffelhiff. "Where's our ship?"

Before the answer came, he added: "An' don't tell me you broke it up and sold the parts."

Hoffelhiff stared sheepishly at Spuckler and took much longer to reply than he should have.

"You drive a hard bargain. I'll give you thirty percent of both sales."

Chapter 12

As the sun broke over the Moonguzzit Sea, Spuckler, Mr. Beeba, Poog, Gax (or what little of Gax we had), and I were shooting across the waves in a decommissioned fogglenaut. Hoffelhiff had given it to us—along with a quick breakfast of boiled bognut meal—after confessing that he'd sold our ship to a scrap dealer who'd crushed it down to the size of a lunch box even before leaving the island.

"Not to worry," he'd said as we climbed aboard and prepared to set sail, "you should be able to reach all three of those buyers before the day is out. Two days, tops."

This would have been reassuring coming from

anyone else, but by this point I'd learned that Hoffel-hiff had a nasty habit of making things sound simpler than they actually were. I asked Mr. Beeba how long he thought it would *really* take to retrieve all of Gax's parts: neck, body, and wheels.

"It would be folly to attempt an accurate estimate at this stage, Akiko," said Mr. Beeba. "Let's just see if we can save Gax's neck for the time being." Then he chuckled and said: "Did you catch that, Akiko? Save his neck. It's a pun."

I rolled my eyes and pretended I hadn't heard him. "So where are we headed first, Spuckler?" I asked.

"The village of Bwibblington," said Spuckler. "Just up the coast a spell. Hoffelhiff says he sold Gax's neck to a little old lady who lives there." He paused and let out a long, sad sigh. "I jus' hope she didn't turn around an' sell it to someone else." I had a sudden, terrible vision of us racing around Smoo for the rest of our lives, Gax's various components always just out of reach.

"I've got an idea," I said. "What if we go some-where and buy a *new* neck for Gax?"

Mr. Beeba gasped. Spuckler's jaw dropped. Poog stared at me with stunned, glassy eyes. And Gax, whose head I had been entrusted with holding in my lap, shivered audibly.

"BUT MA'AM," said Gax. "MY NECK IS MY NECK. A NEW NECK WOULD BE . . . SOME *OTHER* ROBOT'S NECK."

"Yeah, but . . . ," I said, before realizing that I had somehow stumbled into a very emotional topic for Spuckler and Gax. Indeed, for all of us.

Gax needed to be reconstructed as he had been before, *exactly* as he had been before. Not for tech-nical reasons. Not even for sentimental reasons. Just because, well . . . just because it was the right thing to do. You don't take shortcuts when it comes to friends. If you do, then what kind of friend are you?

"BUT *WHAT,* MA'AM?"

I looked Gax in the eye and nodded slowly. "But nothing," I said. "Shift it into high gear, Spuckler. The sooner we get there, the better."

By the time we got to Bwibblington, the sun was well above the horizon, and the sky was a cloudless, dazzling shade of blue. Though not as dramatic as Gollarondo, Bwibblington was remarkable in its own way. It was what Mr. Beeba called a bridge village. There were a number of them on Smoo: villages that had sprung up around an important bridge, thereby guaranteeing visitors and commerce. Bwibblington was unusual in that its location—the shoreline being composed of sheer cliff faces, with little in the way of level land

anywhere nearby—had forced the village planners to build Bwibblington, in its entirety, on the bridge itself.

"Here, Beebs," said Spuckler, handing Mr. Beeba one of the crudely drawn maps Nugg von Hoffelhiff had given to us. "Find out which one of them shacks up there b'longs to Mrs. Wimmaneen Slarf."

"Let's see. Seven four twee Pinnary Lane," said Mr. Beeba, raising the map until it obscured most of his face. "Shouldn't be so hard to find."

"Seven four twee?" I said. "What's *twee* supposed to mean?"

"Twee?" said Mr. Beeba. "Akiko, you're in the sixth grade now. Surely you know the number twee. Should have learned it back in kindergarten, I daresay."

"The number ... *twee*." I drew my eyebrows tightly together. "Where I come from, Mr. Beeba, I'm pretty sure there *is* no number twee."

"Oh, but there's *got* to be," said Mr. Beeba. "It's the number between two and three." He gave me a pitying stare, as if I'd been deprived of one of human civilization's greatest advances. "Twee."

I shrugged and said: "I think we just call it two and a half."

"Two and a half?" said Mr. Beeba. He shuddered and turned his attention back to the map. "How clunky."

Minutes later we arrived at a dock directly below the village, got out of our fogglenaut, and climbed the rickety wooden stairway that led to Bwibblington. As we got closer, we passed several Bwibblingtonians. They were small people, most no more than four feet tall. They had pale gray-blue skin, very widely spaced eyes, and as far as I could see, no nose whatsoever. They all bowed and said "Safe crossing" to us as they passed. The local greeting, Poog explained.

"IT'S HERE," said Gax when we reached the village. "MY NECK IS DEFINITELY HERE. AND IN GOOD WORKING CONDITION."

I lifted Gax's head in both hands and looked into his eyes. "How do you know that, Gax?"

"THERE ARE SMALL HOMING DEVICES IN EACH OF MY BODY PARTS," said Gax.

"Installed 'em myself," said Spuckler proudly, "for just such an occasion."

"UNFORTUNATELY, THE SIGNALS THEY SEND OUT ARE WEAK AND DON'T TRAVEL MORE THAN A FEW HUNDRED FEET," said Gax. "BUT AS I NEAR THE HOMING DEVICES I AM ABLE TO COMMUNICATE QUITE CLEARLY WITH THEM. WITH EFFORT I CAN EVEN MAKE THEM OBEY MY COMMANDS."

A kind merchant directed us to Pinnary Lane, and soon we were standing at the house marked seven four twee. The numeral for *twee*, by the way, looks like this:

$$\zeta$$

I held my breath and rang the doorbell.

PEEM POAM

Before long we heard footsteps coming to the door.

Maybe we'll get lucky and everything will go smoothly, I thought. *We're overdue for some good luck, aren't we?*

Chapter 13

The door creaked open and there stood a hunched old woman with a cane, so wrinkled and frail looking I feared the next gust of wind that blew down Pinnary Lane might carry her away and out to sea. She had a tiny hooked nose (Bwibblingtonian noses emerged only with age, it seemed), incredibly thick glasses, and wispy white hair that looked like fluff from a cottonwood tree.

"Safe crossing," she said, squinting and blinking at us. She didn't look like someone who got visitors very often.

"Safe crossing, madame," said Mr. Beeba. "Do forgive this abrupt and unheralded visit. I sincerely hope that we have not called upon you at a disadvantageous moment, drawing you away from importunate personal affairs, or, heaven forbid, rousing you during a moment of well-earned tranquil repose."

Wimmaneen Slarf coughed and adjusted her glasses. "Speak normal," she said.

I stifled a laugh as Mr. Beeba cleared his throat.

"I, er"—he cleared it again—"hope this isn't a bad time."

Mrs. Slarf blinked several times. "Bad time for what?"

"Yes, well . . ." Mr. Beeba tapped the fingers of both hands together. "Perhaps I'd better just get to the point."

"Ya can say *that* again," said Spuckler.

"Ahem." Mr. Beeba took Gax's head from my hands and showed it to Mrs. Slarf. "I believe that you are in possession of a robotic neck that was, until very recently, attached to this Gax unit."

"Nope," she said.

"Splendid," said Mr. Beeba. "I am prepared to offer you double the price you—" Mr. Beeba stopped talking and blinked in a way that made him look surprisingly similar to Mrs. Slarf. "Did you say no?"

"Nope," she said. "I said nope."

Mr. Beeba took a step back, as if Mrs. Slarf's words had knocked him in the chest. "Do you mean to say you do not have this Gax unit's neck?"

"I don't just *mean* to say it," she replied. "I'm *saying* it."

"But . . ." Mr. Beeba was so taken aback he began several sentences in rapid succession, abandoning each after the first word. "You . . . Yesterday . . . Surely . . ." He stamped his feet with frustration. "Master Hoffelhiff . . ."

"Oh!" said Mrs. Slarf, her eyebrows rising. "That thing I bought at Hoffelhiff's yesterday. It's a robot's neck, is it?"

I stepped forward. "That's right. So you've got it, huh?"

"Well," she said, "yes and no. Here, follow me." She led us around to the back of the house. "It's on my property. But it doesn't belong to me anymore. I gave it to Fofo as a birthday gift." We all went through a narrow alleyway, turned a corner, and stepped into Mrs. Slarf's backyard. "She's become real fond of it, actually."

There, sitting alone on an oversized cushion in one corner of the yard, was a furry pink creature about the size of a guinea pig. She had large elephant-ish ears, almond-shaped eyes with long eyelashes, and a short fluffy tail. Under her front paws was a crooked length of metal with wires hanging out of each end: Mrs. Slarf's backyard pet was resting its feet on Gax's neck.

Spuckler stepped forward to grab it but was stopped by Mrs. Slarf's cane. "Not so fast, shaggy-hair!" Small as she was, Mrs. Slarf sounded surprisingly tough, and Spuckler moved back.

"Now," Mrs. Slarf said, turning her attention to Mr. Beeba. "What was that you were saying about double the price?"

"Of course, of course," said Mr. Beeba, pulling a billfold out from under his belt. "It is my understanding that you paid twenty gilpots for our robot's neck. I will happily offer you forty gilpots to buy it back."

"Make it a hundred and you've got yourself a deal." Mrs. Slarf smiled at Mr. Beeba with all seven of her teeth.

"One hundred!" Mr. Beeba was outraged. "That's *five times* what you paid for it. Just *yesterday*!"

"Beebs," growled Spuckler, "time's a-wastin'. Fork over the dough an' let's skedaddle."

Mr. Beeba groaned as he counted out the money. "Daylight banditry," he muttered as he handed Mrs. Slarf a wad of bills. (I smiled, wondering if Nugg von Hoffelhiff would approve of the use of the word *banditry* in this context. Mrs. Slarf was armed only with shrewdness, but hey, maybe that's the most important weapon of all.)

"Nice doing business with you. It's all yours," said Mrs. Slarf as she went into her house. Before she closed the door, she poked her head back out and said: "Try not to make a mess."

If I'd paid better attention, I would have noticed that "try not to make a mess" was a pretty strange thing to say to people who wanted to take a piece of metal away from a cute little furry animal.

Then again, if I'd paid better attention, I'd have realized that she wasn't talking to us in the first place.

She was talking to Fofo.

Chapter 14

"One down, two to go," said Spuckler as he stepped forward, bent down, and picked up one end of Gax's neck. Fofo made a soft purring sound and happily clamped her tiny mouth around the other end. When Spuckler stood up straight, he found that he was carrying not only Gax's neck, but also Fofo, who was hanging happily from it by her teeth, like a puppy dangling from an oversized bone.

"Heh, heh. Playful critter, ain'tcha?" Spuckler scratched Fofo under her chin. "Sorry to run off with your breakfast, li'l lady, but we gotta vamoose, and we ain't takin' you with us."

Spuckler grabbed hold of Fofo's tail and tried to

pull her off Gax's neck, but Fofo was very firmly attached, and determined not to let go.

Poog made a loud, gurgly announcement, and we all turned to Mr. Beeba for the translation. "Poog says that this little creature is a rather more formidable opponent than she appears to be. It would be highly unwise to antagonize her."

"DO BE CAREFUL, SIR," said Gax, buzzing nervously in my hands. "IF NOT FOR YOUR OWN SAKE, THEN FOR THE SAKE OF MY NECK."

"Well, if you all got any better ideas for gettin' the li'l sucker offa this thing"—Spuckler stopped pulling on Fofo's tail and closed his fingers around her body—"I'd appreciate hearin' 'em."

Fofo was now purring in a way that was less playful than before. In fact, I think it had crossed the line from purr to growl.

"Let go, ya crazy li'l varmint!" said Spuckler, yanking this way and that in mounting frustration. "We're on a schedule here!"

"Spuckler," I said, trying to keep my eyes on

Fofo's body as it swung from side to side, "y-you'd better take it easy. I think Fofo's"—I swallowed hard—"getting *bigger*."

Spuckler stopped for a moment and held Gax's neck before his eyes. Sure enough, Fofo had expanded in both length and girth. She was now as big as a good-sized raccoon and—more disturbingly— had somehow acquired bigger, sharper teeth in the process.

"A folvering quog-nat," said Mr. Beeba, his voice trembling with either fascination or terror (probably both). "I've read of them before but never seen one up close."

"Well, whatever she is," said Spuckler, raising Gax's neck high into the air so that Fofo teetered precariously at the very top of it, "she's about to get some flyin' lessons, Spuck style."

"No!" shouted Mr. Beeba and I simultaneously.

But it was too late: Spuckler had started whipping Fofo around and around and around in an attempt to fling her into the air, spinning her like some sort of enormous living noisemaker. With every spin Fofo grew larger and more muscular.

"MY NECK" was all Gax could say. He had reason to wonder if it would survive the ordeal. Fofo was already as big as a German shepherd and showed no sign of halting her sudden growth spurt.

All was a blur as Spuckler whirled with tornado-like fervor, pouring every ounce of strength he had into the effort. When he finally slowed to a stop, dizzy and exhausted, Fofo was precisely where she'd been at the start, with one important difference: she was now the size of a fully grown lion, and every bit as ferocious looking. She let out a thunderously loud roar and planted her muscular legs firmly on the ground.

Gax's neck was in surprisingly good shape (I guess Gax units really *are* the toughest little 'bots in the universe). Spuckler, on the other hand, was looking a good deal the worse for wear. He was panting, coughing, and wheezing and—now on all fours—had actually let go of Gax's neck altogether.

"Oh dear," said Mr. Beeba.

Against all expectations, Fofo then released Gax's saliva-drenched neck from her teeth and let it thud to the ground in front of her. She was panting cheerfully, her massive tongue hanging out one side of her mouth. She looked like a dog that wanted to play fetch.

Spuckler rose up on his elbows and eyed Gax's neck hungrily. It was well within arm's reach, but so were Fofo's formidable jaws.

"Don't do it, Spuckler," said Mr. Beeba. "It's a trap."

"I can snag it, Beebs," said Spuckler. "I'm fast enough. *Plenty* fast enough."

"No, Spuckler," I said. "Fofo's too close. She'll bite your arm off!"

There was an excruciating silence as Spuckler and Fofo maintained their positions, neither of them moving forward, neither of them backing down. They were like gunslingers at high noon. All that was missing was the tumbleweed.

"IF YOU CAN WAIT JUST ANOTHER MINUTE, SIR," said Gax, "I BELIEVE I WILL BE ABLE TO FACILITATE THE PROCESS."

"We ain't got another minute, Gax," said Spuckler between clenched teeth. "It's now or never."

"THIRTY MORE SECONDS, SIR," said Gax. "THAT'S ALL I NEED."

"Sorry, Gax."

It happened in a flash, in a blaze of movement that was barely perceivable: Spuckler leaping forward . . . grabbing Gax's neck . . . Fofo lunging . . . her mouth drawing open . . . wider, wider, and wider still . . . Spuckler looking up only when it was too late . . . and then, incredibly, impossibly, sickeningly . . . Fofo's enormous mouth rushed forward like an ocean wave . . . swept over Spuckler . . . and closed around the entire upper half of his body.

"No!" I cried, tossing Gax's head to the ground and scrambling forward to grab hold of Spuckler's

leg. Mr. Beeba grabbed the other leg, and we both pulled as hard as we could.

An earsplitting stream of warbly gurgles filled the air as Poog unleashed a series of incantations presumably designed to throw Fofo back on her heels. But Fofo was a force of nature beyond even Poog's powers, and the best Poog could manage was to slow the progress of Fofo's jaws as they inched past Spuckler's waist.

"Harder!" I cried, pulling with all my might even as Fofo gulped her way down Spuckler's thighs.

Mr. Beeba was panicked beyond words, his face bathed in sweat and contorted into an expression of boundless terror. "We're . . . we're *losing* him!"

Poog's voice grew high-pitched and shrill, the gurgly syllables blasting from his mouth in an endless torrent.

ULK-ULK-ULK-ULK

Fofo lunged past Spuckler's knees in a final bid to swallow him whole. I thrust my arms up to

Spuckler's calf. My forearms were now entirely inside Fofo's mouth, and the rivers of saliva made it almost impossible to maintain my grip. Mr. Beeba was faring no better and had begun whimpering like a child. I pulled as hard as I possibly could, digging my nails into Spuckler's leg in a last-ditch effort to hang on, but . . .

GUGGLE-GUGGLE-GUK!

. . . Fofo's lips closed around Spuckler's ankles, forcing Mr. Beeba and me to let go. We both watched in horror as Fofo sucked Spuckler all the way in like a strand of spaghetti and . . .

SSSLLLURRRRRT!

. . . he was gone.

"Spuckler!" I screamed, my eyes wide in disbelief.

There were several agonizing seconds of motionlessness as Mr. Beeba and I stared helplessly at Fofo's mouth while her tongue slithered back and forth over her lips in triumph. Poog's incantations slowed, grew quiet and uncertain, then petered out altogether. Fofo parted her lips for a surprisingly dainty burp, and Spuckler's doom seemed utter and complete.

Then . . .

. . . somewhere deep inside Fofo . . .

. . . there was a muffled *POP* . . .

. . . a *FFFT* . . .

. . . and a *ZZRRRITCH* of electricity.

A second of silence, then . . .

ZUP-ZUP-ZUP-ZUP-ZUP-ZUP-ZUP

. . . Fofo's lips peeled back and her jaws flew open wide. Spuckler somersaulted out of her mouth and plopped onto the ground in a splattery, saliva-covered mess. He was still clutching Gax's neck in his hands, only now it was a living creature, writhing back and forth, sparks shooting out one end and smoke billowing out the other.

In a matter of seconds Fofo lost all the size and ferocity she had gained over the course of the battle, and returned to her original small and harmless state. She moaned ruefully and bounded through a flap in Mrs. Slarf's back door, like a cat that had been smacked hard with a rolled-up newspaper.

Only then did I turn to see Gax's head, upside down on the ground, rocking back and forth in exhaustion. As promised, he had facilitated the process with—I now understood—a remotely triggered burst of electricity deep inside Fofo's throat at the last possible moment. Leave it to Gax to save his own neck and that of his master at the same time.

"Tsk, tsk, tsk."

It was Mrs. Slarf, stroking Fofo's fur and staring down at Spuckler from a second-story window overlooking the backyard. Or rather, she was staring at the pool of saliva in which Spuckler was seated.

"Fofo, girl," she said disapprovingly. "I thought I told you not to make a mess."

Chapter 15

Within half an hour we were back in the foggle-naut and sailing away from Bwibblington at top speed. Mr. Beeba manned the controls while Spuckler reattached Gax's neck to the base of his head. Gax was still a very long way from complete—he looked more like a discarded desk lamp than a full-fledged robot—but the addition of his neck made a surprisingly big difference. We were making progress, at least, and Gax was just that much closer to being his old self again.

"I reckon I owe ya one there, Gax," said Spuckler. "If I hadn't been holdin' your neck, I'd be a nice big bucket of Fofo chow right now."

"YOU'RE TOO KIND, SIR," said Gax, wagging his neck back and forth like a newly acquired tail. "I AM CERTAIN YOU'D HAVE FOUND A WAY OUT OF YOUR PREDICAMENT EVENTUALLY."

"Don't be so sure, Gax," Mr. Beeba said. "When it comes to predicaments, Spuckler is far better at getting in than getting out."

"So where are we going now?" I asked. "And which part of Gax are we going to find there?"

"Next on the list is Gax's body," said Mr. Beeba. "It has been purchased by a scientist on the island of Vorf, not so very far from here. A fellow by the name of Gridstump."

"A scientist, eh?" I said, turning to Gax. "Jeez, I hope he's not performing weird experiments on your body."

"I SUPPOSE HE COULD BE," replied Gax, "BUT I DOUBT IT. MORE LIKELY HE IS SIMPLY MAKING USE OF THE EQUIPMENT WITHIN THE HULL. AS YOU MAY RE-CALL, THERE ARE A GREAT NUMBER OF USEFUL TOOLS CONCEALED WITHIN MY BODY."

I thought back to that night we were in the Sprubly Islands, when I had started pushing buttons on Gax in hopes of getting a torch. I couldn't help chuckling as I recalled all the things I had gotten instead: a boxing glove, a bicycle horn, a bottle of window spray.

"Who knows," I said to Gax with a wink, "maybe your body will have knocked the guy out with the boxing glove by the time we catch up with him."

"IT'S ENTIRELY POSSIBLE, MA'AM," said Gax with a hint of pride.

After an hour or two spent crossing the choppy waves of the Moonguzzit Sea, the island of Vorf came into view. It was dominated by an enormous mountain that cast a menacing black shadow on the horizon. I'd say it was like Mount Fuji, except Fuji is majestic and snowcapped, whereas this thing was monstrous, ugly, and capped with nothing but charred black volcanic rock. Add the fact that several plumes of thick black smoke were billowing from its peak, and we're not exactly talking about something you'd buy postcards of (unless you're

looking for postcards to mail to members of a biker gang or a punk rock band).

"Mount Vorf," said Mr. Beeba. "Not to worry: it's very nearly extinct."

"*Very nearly* extinct?" I asked. "Isn't that the same as *not quite* extinct?"

"Oh no, Akiko," said Mr. Beeba. "Far from it.

Very nearly extinct is much more along the lines of *won't erupt unless we are almost unimaginably unlucky*."

I decided to let it drop, even though *unimaginably unlucky* seemed the perfect description of everything that had happened to us since this whole trip had started.

Mr. Beeba guided the fogglenaut up to a small dock and we all climbed out. A wide stretch of pitch-black sand separated us from a bank of smoke-tinged palm trees and scraggly gray grass.

"Well, we've got one thing working in our favor this time," said Mr. Beeba. "Dr. Gridstump is the only living soul on this island, so we're not likely to confuse him with anyone else."

"Let's just find him and get this over with," I said. "The sooner we get off this island, the better."

But before we could even set foot on the beach, we were halted by an ominous announcement from Poog, who had returned to the spot where our fogglenaut was roped to the dock.

"Good heavens," said Mr. Beeba after joining

Poog, who was inspecting a number of slimy gray eel-like creatures attached to the side of the fogglenaut. "Hurpleskaps. Dozens of them!"

"Man alive," said Spuckler. "They're gonna sink the thing in no time."

"These creatures spell doom for any seafaring vessel," said Mr. Beeba. "Or anything made out of metal, for that matter. They secrete an acidic substance that eats through the hulls of ships in a matter of minutes."

Poog had begun a series of quiet incantations designed to lure the eels away from our fogglenaut. Sure enough, after several seconds, the hurpleskaps began to drop off the hull, splash into the water, and swim away. Before long the fogglenaut was entirely free of the "dagnabbed little steel-suckers" (as Spuckler called them).

Poog paused to say something to Mr. Beeba, then returned to his incantations.

"Poog has got the situation well in hand," said Mr. Beeba. "Hurpleskaps are among the many creatures over which he is capable of exerting mind control. Unfortunately, he will have to stay here with the ship to ensure that the hurpleskaps don't return."

"You mean we're"—I looked back and forth between Poog and Mr. Beeba—"splitting up?"

"Unfortunately, yes," said Mr. Beeba. "Poog doesn't like the idea any more than you do, but there's simply no alternative. It won't do us any good to stick together if that means returning to a sunken fogglenaut."

There was no arguing with *that*. So we all bid Poog a temporary farewell and made our way up the beach in search of the island's lone inhabitant.

It didn't take long to find him. There was only one building on the whole island, and its white domed roof stood out in sharp contrast to the blackness of Mount Vorf behind it. As we drew closer to it, it became clear that we were approaching a combination laboratory/observatory.

When we got to the front door, we found that

there was no doorbell, no knocker, nothing at all that we could use to announce our presence. So Spuckler—our resident presence announcer—began yelling, whistling, throwing rocks on the roof, and (almost as an afterthought) pounding on the door with all his might.

Sometime after Spuckler's third barrage of noise calculated to wake the dead, we heard a voice.

"Looking for someone?"

The voice had not come from behind the door. It had come from behind *us*.

We spun around and found ourselves face to face with Dr. Gridstump.

Chapter 16

He was bathed in sweat and was wearing a hat with a thick net hanging off it, the sort of thing you see on beekeepers. In one hand he was holding a giant butterfly net; in the other, a basket filled with an enormous quantity of dead insects: the product, I assumed, of a busy morning studying what little flora and fauna he could find on the island.

But even without all that, he'd have been a very odd man to behold. He looked like he'd been put together by someone who wanted him to fall over: his squareish head was too big for his body, and his chest was too big for his legs. His eyes were so small they vanished beneath his eyebrows, and his nose was almost laughably pointy. His mouth stretched so far across his face it looked as if the upper half of his head were capable of tilting back on a hinge.

"Well, well, well," said Dr. Gridstump, removing his hat and stepping over to Mr. Beeba. "If it isn't the legendary Beeba: genius, philosopher, and man of letters."

Mr. Beeba blushed and broke into a pleased—if slightly confused—smile. "I'm sorry, my dear fellow, but . . . do I know you?"

"Do you?" said Dr. Gridstump, nodding mysteriously. "Do you indeed?" He grinned and raised a long finger. "Maybe you do, old boy. Maybe you don't." He chuckled. "But I know you. Yes, my word, yes. How could I not? Why, you're a legend in these parts."

"I am?" said Mr. Beeba, his smile growing along with his confusion. "Hm, well, I suppose I've . . . er, made a *bit* of a name for myself, yes." He paused, then added: "I *do* know you, don't I? The face is *ever* so familiar. . . ."

"Gridstump," said the man, stepping forward and giving Mr. Beeba's hand a vigorous shaking. "Eckston B. Gridstump, at your service. You and I were at school together. The University of Malbadoo."

"Aaaah!" said Mr. Beeba, in the manner of someone finally having put two and two together. "But of course. How could I have forgotten!" Something in Mr. Beeba's voice didn't quite ring true, though, and I wondered if he had any real memories of this old classmate of his. "Eckston Gridstump. What a pleasure it is to see you again after all these years."

"When Knowledge and Ignorance meet . . . ," said Gridstump.

Mr. Beeba grinned. ". . . let them shake hands and agree to have lunch sometime!" Mr. Beeba turned to me and explained: "The old school motto."

"Yes," said Dr. Gridstump, still shaking Mr. Beeba's hand, "but which of us is Knowledge, and which of us is Ignorance?" He smiled with all his might, his mouth full of slightly yellowed teeth.

Mr. Beeba laughed good-naturedly. "Which, indeed!"

"So tell me, old boy," said Dr. Gridstump as he led Mr. Beeba inside for a guided tour of his laboratory. "What brings you to my island retreat?"

Spuckler and I (carrying Gax's head and neck) followed them indoors. We eventually came to a large, well-lit laboratory filled with all sorts of tables, tools, textbooks, and test tubes. After a bit of small talk about old professors at Malbadoo and the difficulty of finding good litmus paper these days, Mr. Beeba finally brought up the matter of Gax's missing body. As soon as he did, Dr. Gridstump's face lit up with understanding, and he led Mr. Beeba into an adjoining room where he said he'd been storing Gax's body and—just as Gax had predicted— making use of some of its tools.

"I don't know about this guy," I said once Mr. Beeba and Dr. Gridstump had left the room. "He's . . . strange. It's not just that he *looks* funny. He *talks* funny and *acts* funny too."

"Yeah," said Spuckler. "I know just whatcher talkin' about." He paused and added: "And Gridstump's kinda weird too."

I stared at Spuckler, realized he wasn't joking, and decided not to say anything.

"DO YOU THINK DR. GRIDSTUMP IS REALLY THE OLD CLASSMATE HE CLAIMS TO BE?" asked Gax.

"If he is, he certainly didn't make much of an impression on Mr. Beeba."

"People don't make impressions on Beebs," said Spuckler. "He's always too busy doin' crazy math stuff like addiction an' substraption an' multicrustacean." I marveled for a moment that Spuckler had managed to get all three words so thoroughly wrong. "Why, they coulda been sat next to each other for twenny-five years an' Beebs wouldn't've even known the guy was there."

"Shhh," I said. "They're coming back."

"Problem solved!" said Mr. Beeba, beaming from (I assumed) several more generous doses of flattery about his status as an academic legend. Behind him was Dr. Gridstump, who had placed Gax's body on a cart and was now wheeling it into the room. To Gridstump's credit, it looked to be in perfect shape.

"Good old Eckston here tells me he half suspected Gax's body was acquired under dubious circumstances," said Mr. Beeba, "and that its true owner would be along to retrieve it in the fullness of time." Dr. Gridstump nodded cheerfully. "The only reason he bought it, in fact, was to prevent Hoffel-hiff from selling it to a less scrupulous buyer."

"Right," I said, sounding skeptical in spite of my efforts not to. Still, here was Gax's body, and Gridstump was returning it to us. What was there to be suspicious about?

"Eckston and I are going for a brief tour of the island," said Mr. Beeba, his eyes gleaming in anticipation. "It won't take us more than a half hour or so," he added, waving a hand in the direction of Gax's body and turning to Spuckler. "That'll give you a chance to get Gax's neck properly reattached."

"I'm on it, Beebs," said Spuckler, a wrench already in hand.

"I'm going with you," I said to Mr. Beeba. "There's strength in numbers." Dr. Gridstump gave me a *what-is*-that-*supposed-to-mean* look, as did Mr. Beeba. "I mean . . . this island has a *number of strengths* . . ." I fumbled for a way of salvaging the sentence. ". . . that I would like to, er . . . witness firsthand."

"A number of strengths, eh?" said Mr. Beeba.

Dr. Gridstump stepped forward, frowning at the prospect of having anyone join them. "You'd really better stay here. We're going to climb to the summit of Mount Vorf. I'm afraid the path is far too rugged for a mere *girl*."

That did it.

"A *mere girl*?" I said. "What are you saying? That girls are weak?"

"Don't twist the man's words, Akiko," said Mr. Beeba. "I'm sure he only meant to say that girls are dainty, frail, and prone to fainting spells."

"Precisely," said Dr. Gridstump.

My first instinct was to tell them both off. But then it dawned on me: who was to say either of them had to *know* I was tagging along?

"You know what? You're right," I said, raising my hands in a gesture of acceptance. "I *am* pretty dainty and frail, come to think of it. I'll just stay behind and"—I smiled as innocently as I knew how—"keep out of trouble."

"A sensible choice," said Mr. Beeba. "Have a rest, dear child. And don't worry," he added, having sensed my unease with the situation. "We're only hiking to the top of a semiactive volcano. What could possibly go wrong?"

Chapter 17

I saw them out the front door of the laboratory, waving goodbye as they began the hike. Then, after telling Spuckler and Gax what I was up to, I followed Mr. Beeba and Dr. Gridstump from a distance.

It was a steep and grueling climb. Once or twice I made a bit too much noise scrambling from one outcropping of volcanic rock to another, and Dr. Gridstump nearly caught on. Fortunately, he was so intent on getting Mr. Beeba to the summit of Mount Vorf that he wasn't inclined to delay their ascent by snooping around for me.

Finally we reached the summit: a hazy, hot region devoid of anything living, apart from a handful of smoke-singed trees. The air reeked of sulfur and smoke. Everything I touched—the rocks, the ground, the sand—gave off heat like an oven.

I watched from behind a nearby boulder as Gridstump led Mr. Beeba to the edge of a depression at the top of this "very nearly extinct" volcano. Their faces were bathed from beneath with an orange glow, and I knew at once that they were gazing down into a pit of molten lava.

"Magnificent, isn't it?" said Dr. Gridstump. "As a man of science, I knew you'd want to have a look at this."

fffFFFFFFRRRRGGHHFFFfffff

A fiery ball of magma shot over their heads and into the branches of a nearby tree, which promptly exploded into flame.

"Y-yes," replied Mr. Beeba, sounding considerably more nervous than he had earlier. "Volc-c-canoes are ever so fascinating. It's a shame the others aren't here to see it."

"Ah, but I don't bring just anyone up here," said

Dr. Gridstump, patting Mr. Beeba on the back. "Only those who have crossed me at one time or another."

"C-crossed you?" Mr. Beeba was now stumbling backward, away from Dr. Gridstump. "I'm sure I don't know wh-what you mean." I couldn't see the doctor's face from where I was hiding, but one look at Mr. Beeba's expression told me he was no longer gazing into the eyes of a friend.

"But of course you don't." Dr. Gridstump advanced on Mr. Beeba. "Your sort never recall the little people like me. The ones whose lives you've crushed along the way!"

It was clear that Mr. Beeba was in mortal danger; for all I knew he could be seconds from being tossed down into the lava. Still, I couldn't just jump out at random. If I was to have any success taking on Gridstump, I needed to retain the element of surprise and make the best possible use of it.

"You couldn't crush *me*, though." Gridstump was now well within arm's reach of Mr. Beeba, and getting closer with every sentence he muttered. "I went on to become a great scientist. I did it in spite of you. In spite of what you did to me."

Taking a deep breath, I inched my way to the top of a strategically located boulder. From there I would be able to jump down onto the doctor's back at the moment of my choosing.

"But in those days I was a *nobody* to you," said Gridstump to a now thoroughly petrified Mr. Beeba. "Still, that didn't stop you from reporting me to the authorities, did it?"

"The authorities?" Mr. Beeba had now backed himself into a wall of boulders not far from the pit's edge. "At M-Malbadoo?"

"No, not at Malbadoo, you fool!" said Gridstump. "At the *SMATDA*!" He lunged forward and grabbed Mr. Beeba by the neck. "Do you remember me *now*?" He shook Mr. Beeba like a bully shaking a child. *"Do you?"*

Gridstump had taken a few crucial steps away from where I was hiding, and it was no longer a given that I would be able to jump all the way from the boulder to his back. But it was too late to worry about that. I had to make my move.

I rose to my feet and leaped as far as I could from the boulder.

PPFFTCH

Disaster! I completely missed Gridstump and instead took a spectacularly clumsy spill into the patch of stone and sand at his feet. Pain shot through my shoulders as I rolled across it.

Gridstump whirled around, his hands still clamped on to Mr. Beeba's neck. "You!"

So much for jumping on his back. I had to think fast.

I dug the fingers of both hands into the burning hot volcanic sand, picked up as much of it as I could, and hurled both fistfuls straight into Gridstump's eyes.

"Aaarrgghff!"

Gridstump clawed madly at his eyes with one hand, but he still held Mr. Beeba with the other.

"Let go of him!" I cried as I tried to pry his fingers away from Mr. Beeba's throat.

"Never!" growled Gridstump. He now gave up on

trying to clear the sand from his eyes and returned to his two-handed grip on Mr. Beeba's neck. "He wrecked my life! Over a piece of *chewing gum*!"

There had to be some way of freeing Mr. Beeba. Even without his eyesight, Gridstump would eventually get Mr. Beeba to the edge of the pit and it would all be over. But what could I do? I simply didn't have the strength to take on Gridstump all on my own. I needed some kind of weapon, some kind of . . .

The tree!

I ran to the blackened tree that had been struck moments before by the flying ball of lava. The tips of its branches were red-hot and smoldering. I snapped one off, brandished it like a spear, and, dashing back to the scene of the struggle, jabbed it into Gridstump's rear end with all my might.

"Aaaauuuurrrggghh!"

Gridstump was in excruciating pain but had still not let go of Mr. Beeba. To make matters worse, he now had Mr. Beeba teetering at the edge of the pit. There was no time to think. Only to act.

I grabbed Mr. Beeba with one arm, raised the smoldering branch with the other, and jabbed its glowing orange tip as quickly as I could into both of Gridstump's hands.

"Nnnngggh!"

He groaned and let go of Mr. Beeba . . .

. . . for a fraction of a second . . .

. . . and a fraction of a second was all I needed.

I dropped the stick and, using every ounce of strength I had, pulled Mr. Beeba to safety.

Gridstump dropped to his knees and released an anguished howl as Mr. Beeba and I tore off down the trail as fast as our legs would carry us. I like to think he recovered his eyesight just in time to see Mr. Beeba and me vanish into the distance.

"My apologies, Akiko," said Mr. Beeba between hoarsely gasped breaths as we ran nonstop all the way down the mountainside.

"You . . ."

hnnh hnnh

". . . are not . . ."

hnnh hnnh

". . . the least bit . . ."

hnnh hnnh

". . . dainty."

Chapter 18

Minutes later we arrived back at the lab. Gax was now almost his old self again, but there was little time to celebrate. Gridstump would recover soon enough and be back down with who-knew-what plan for getting revenge on Mr. Beeba. We left one hundred and fifty gilpots—the amount Gridstump had paid for Gax's robotic body—on one of the worktables and ran back to the fogglenaut at top speed, Spuckler carrying Gax all the way.

As we piled into the fogglenaut, joined by Poog, who looked very happy to be relieved of his de-hurpleskapping duties, Mount Vorf proved just how unextinct it really was by erupting, sending lava spraying hundreds of feet skyward in slow motion. Balls of liquid fire shot through the air like rockets, pelting the beach and making huge steamy splashes in the Moonguzzit Sea.

Just before we shut the door of the fogglenaut, I saw Dr. Gridstump arrive on the beach with what looked like an enormous bazooka on his shoulders.

FffffFFFRROOOOOOOSHHH!

Spuckler gunned the fogglenaut just in time, and off we went, cutting through the waves at top speed and leaving a very angry Dr. Gridstump on the dock, firing wildly at us with his weapon long after we were no longer in range.

I watched through the fogglenaut's back window as the island of Vorf receded into the distance, my heartbeat gradually slowing from a rapid pounding to something pretty close to normal. By the time the smoke from Mount Vorf disappeared into the horizon, I was sound asleep.

* * *

When I awoke, it was nearly nightfall.

"Somebody please tell me," I said, yawning and stretching, "that Gax's wheels will be easier to get hold of than his neck and body were."

"As a matter of fact," said Mr. Beeba, "we've been discussing that very topic while you rested, and we have reached a decision that I expect will come as a great relief to you."

"What's that?"

"We're going to give up on retrieving Gax's wheels and head back to Gollarondo." Mr. Beeba smiled and patted me on the hand. "You've gone through more than enough trouble already, my dear girl, on my account as well as Gax's." A tear had come into Mr. Beeba's eye, and he wiped it away with a shaking finger. "Why, you risked your very *life* to save me, Akiko."

"That's right, 'Kiko," said Spuckler, leaving the fogglenaut on autopilot and coming back to join the discussion, "and believe you me, Beebs ain't worth that kind of sacrifice."

"Quite right," said Mr. Beeba.

"Heck, he ain't even worth breakin' your limbs for, really."

"Indeed."

"Or even stubbin' your big toe for, come to think of it."

"Ahem," said Mr. Beeba, keeping his eyes focused on mine. "Akiko, I cannot in good conscience allow you to put yourself in harm's way again. Spuckler and I did promise you, after all, no near-death experiences on this trip."

"But . . ." I was stunned for some reason, rather than relieved. "But what about Gax's wheels?"

"WE'RE GOING TO BUY A SET OF NEW ONES INSTEAD," said Gax, who—there was no denying it—looked pretty much complete as is. "THE ONES THAT ARE MISSING WERE RATHER SCUFFED AND TIMEWORN ANYWAY. THEY WERE OVERDUE FOR REPLACEMENT, IT MUST BE SAID."

Poog floated over to my side and spoke softly in Toogolian.

"Poog assures you it's for the best, Akiko," said Mr. Beeba. "There are points in any noble pursuit at which the risks exceed the benefits. We are presently at just such a juncture, and there is no shame in playing it safe."

I should have been happy. No, make that *ecstatic*. My scrape with Dr. Gridstump had left me very rattled (not to mention thoroughly exhausted), and the prospect of spending the rest of my time on Smoo just taking it easy should have struck me as heavenly.

But something was wrong. Something about it just didn't *feel* right.

"Now hang on a second," I said.

"Yes?" said Mr. Beeba.

"Don't *I* get a say in this decision?"

Spuckler, Mr. Beeba, Poog, and Gax all exchanged a quick series of embarrassed glances.

"Course ya do, 'Kiko," said Spuckler, eliciting nods from the others. "Your 'pinion's just as important as anybody's."

"Good," I said. "Because I think I'm the only one here who hasn't completely flipped out."

A stunned silence.

"I mean, listen to yourselves. What was that you said, Spuckler, about Mr. Beeba not being worth the sacrifice? You should be ashamed." Spuckler rubbed his jaw. "He's a member of this group, and that means he's worth *any* sacrifice.

"And you, Gax," I continued. "Yeah, all right, maybe those wheels had been around the track one too many times . . . and okay, maybe you didn't have the tires balanced and rotated as often as you could have"—Spuckler nodded, accepting some of the blame—"but you wore them with style. They looked *good* on you, those tires." Gax straightened up and raised his head. "*Darn* good.

"And you two." I turned to Mr. Beeba and Poog. "What is all this talk about giving up and playing it safe? I've never heard you guys talk that way before." I paused and thought about it a bit more. "Well, okay, I've heard Mr. *Beeba* talk that way before," I admitted. "A *lot*. But Poog," I added, raising a finger, "never."

All eyes were on me.

"I say we put it to a vote."

I unbuckled my seat belt and stood up. I don't know why, exactly. I just did it.

"All those in favor of throwing in the towel and running away with our tails between our legs, say aye."

"Ah—" said Mr. Beeba before realizing that no one was joining him. "Ah . . . ah . . ." He then threw both hands over his face and did the most pathetically unconvincing fake sneeze I've ever heard in my life. ". . . CHOO!" Everyone looked at Mr. Beeba through half-closed eyelids. "Excuse me," said Mr. Beeba, wiping imaginary runniness from his nose.

"Gesundheit," I said, looking heavenward. "Let's try that again: anyone here who is too scared, too weak-kneed, and, yes, too *dainty* to carry on with this mission, say aye."

Silence.

"All those who say we will not rest . . ." I looked everyone in the eye, one at a time. ". . . will not cave . . . will not so much as *flinch* in the face of certain *death*"—a little over the top, I know, but, hey, I was on a roll—". . . until we've got Gax's tires fully inflated and back where they belong . . ." Mouths were already open, waiting for my cue. ". . . say aye."

"AYE!" cried everyone at once, loud and clear (except Poog, who cried the equivalent in Toogolian).

"All right, then," I said, strapping myself into my seat and waving Spuckler back to the steering wheel. "Turn this fogglenaut around and step on the gas, already. We've got some wheels to find!"

Chapter 19

As little as we'd known about the buyers of Gax's neck and body, we knew even less about the man or woman or alien or who knows what who'd bought Gax's wheels.

"Unfortunately, the details are rather more sketchy than in the cases of Mrs. Slarf and Dr. Gridstump," said Mr. Beeba. "Hoffelhiff said that he sold Gax's wheels to someone representing a mysterious parts dealer in the metropolis of Omega Doy Zarius. The dealer goes by the name Thirgen, and is known to frequent an establishment known as the Stripped Gear. That's all we know, I'm afraid."

"Well, it's better than nothing," I said. "If we can

get to the Stripped Gear, chances are someone there will know who we're looking for."

"Let's hope so." But after our brush with Dr. Gridstump, I'll bet Mr. Beeba was more than half hoping we'd never cross paths with Thirgen, whoever he'd turn out to be.

In the late afternoon we entered a large bay surrounded by a vast cityscape of shimmering futuristic buildings. "Omega Doy Zarius," said Spuckler, his eyes bugging with excitement. "It ain't changed a bit."

It was a city on the scale of Hong Kong—make that *several* Hong Kongs—and looked to be just as crowded and hectic. Skyscrapers towered like enormous glass and steel steeples, only to be dwarfed by other skyscrapers surrounding them. Roaring rocket ships big and small sped from place to place, coming perilously close to the sides of buildings and one another. Seafaring vessels, most many times larger than our tiny fogglenaut, sounded their horns as they sailed past on all sides, occasionally allowing a glimpse of rusting robots and multicolored aliens manning their controls. Screechings and clankings and oily smells rushed forth to greet me (or drive me away, more accurately), and I found myself hoping our stay in Omega Doy Zarius would be the shortest of our visits.

Mr. Beeba pulled our fogglenaut up to one of the smaller docks and paid an attendant—who assured us this section of the bay was free of hurpleskaps—to keep an eye on it for us. Then we all climbed out and made our way onto one of Omega Doy Zarius's insanely busy streets. After Mr. Beeba failed to get the attention of any of the black and yellow hover taxis that periodically zoomed past, Spuckler set Gax on the ground and promised to show us "how it's done." The very next hover taxi that roared along did indeed come to a complete stop, but only after Spuckler had thrown himself onto the windshield, forcing the driver to plow headlong into a nearby newspaper stand. Mr. Beeba angrily compensated the newspaper salesman for his lost copies of the *Daily Skraboosh,* and off we went.

One brief (but thoroughly hair-raising) hover-taxi ride later, we arrived in the middle of Omega Doy Zarius's machinery district. It was, if anything, even noisier and stinkier than the rest of the city. Spuckler had actually been to the Stripped Gear once before, and after a good half hour of hunting through dozens of crowded streets and steamy back alleys, he delivered us safely to its grime-stained double doors.

Stepping through those doors was like stumbling into a poker party in some strange alien basement: it was dark and smoky and reeked of last week's carryout. Sitar-like music blared from a spherical jukebox, and an enormous fish tank on one wall filled the room with spooky blue-green shadows. It was hard to see any more than the silhouettes of the creatures that were in the place, but at least half had eyes on stalks sprouting out of their faces, and several of them were so tall their oblong heads smacked against the ceiling every time they laughed.

Spuckler got a table and ordered an enormous amount of food for each of us. It was easily the most disgustingly greasy slop I'd ever encountered in my life, but I gratefully devoured it anyway, having not had a bite since the bowl of bognut meal at Hoffelhiff's. When the waiter brought the bill, Spuckler asked if he'd seen a pal of his called Thirgen in the place recently.

"A pal of yours?" said the waiter. "Some pal. He's sittin' right *behind* ya, buddy!"

We all turned our heads to see who the waiter was referring to, but there was no one behind Spuckler apart from a couple of robots chatting with one another in the corner.

Mr. Beeba eyed the Gax-like robot on the left. "But of *course*. The absolute ideal customer for the item in question, come to think of it."

"You mean . . . ," I began.

"Precisely," said Mr. Beeba. "Thirgen is neither a

humanoid nor an alien. He's a robot." He paused and added: "And a Gax unit, at that."

Spuckler and Mr. Beeba immediately began arguing over who would handle the delicate matter of negotiating with Thirgen. Spuckler claimed he knew the lay of the land in Omega Doy Zarius better than any of us, whereas Mr. Beeba insisted Spuckler's impulsive behavior at Mrs. Slarf's place had disqualified him from all future dealings "with civilized society, robotic or otherwise." Finally I proposed that Gax handle things, since he would be able to converse with Thirgen as one Gax unit to another.

"An inspired suggestion, Akiko," said Mr. Beeba. "What do you say, Gax?"

"I THOUGHT YOU'D NEVER ASK." Gax tipped his head back and let out an indignant squeak. "I'D BE DELIGHTED TO."

Spuckler picked up Gax and stepped cautiously over to Thirgen and his robot friend. Gax straightened up as best he could and, in the custom of robots, got their attention with a few beeps and whistles and a well-timed *boop*.

"FORGIVE ME IF I AM MISTAKEN," said Gax, "BUT ARE YOU NOT THE ILLUSTRIOUS GAX UNIT KNOWN AS THIRGEN?"

Thirgen turned to face us and I got my first good look at him. He was similar to Gax—well, pre-dismantled Gax, at any rate—but with a number of important differences. He was older than Gax, and

far more beat-up and battered. He rattled and squeaked with every move, and looked ready to break down at any moment. I felt that we were looking at a kindly old grandpa version of Gax: what Gax would look like when the stress and strain of daily life required him to move more slowly, and when his most vital components were on the verge of giving out for good.

"I AM INDEED," said Thirgen, teetering unsteadily toward us. "WITH WHOM DO I HAVE THE PLEASURE OF COMMUNICATING?" I breathed a quiet sigh of relief. After the dangers of dealing with Fofo and Dr. Gridstump, it seemed we had finally found someone quiet and gentle to work with.

"I AM GAX-62-381," said Gax, using his full name for the very first time (while *I* was within earshot, anyway). "IT IS AN HONOR TO MAKE YOUR ACQUAINTANCE."

"MY CONDOLENCES ON YOUR MISHAP," said Thirgen, having noticed Gax's lack of wheels. "I WISH YOU A SPEEDY RECONSTITUTION."

"THANK YOU, GOOD SIR," said Gax. "AS IT HAP-
PENS, I BELIEVE YOU WILL BE ABLE TO HELP ME IN
THAT REGARD."

A look of understanding came into Thirgen's robotic eyes. "OH NO. PLEASE SAY IT ISN'T SO." He pro-
duced an agitated buzz and rolled back a few inches
on his wheels. "NOT THOSE WHEELS I BOUGHT YES-
TERDAY. THE SALESMAN ASSURED MY PURCHASING
AGENT THEY WERE DISCARDED."

"I AM SURE YOU AND YOUR PURCHASING AGENT
ARE ENTIRELY BLAMELESS IN THE AFFAIR," said Gax.
"BE THAT AS IT MAY . . ."

"NOT ANOTHER WORD, MY MECHANICAL BROTHER,"
said Thirgen, rolling forward and patting Gax on the
helmet with a quivering robotic arm. "THOSE WHEELS
ARE YOURS, AND I WOULD NO SOONER KEEP THEM
FROM YOU THAN HAVE MY VERY OWN CARBURETOR
TORN FROM MY HULL." He apologized to his robot
friend for breaking short their meeting, then turned
his attention back to us. "PLEASE FOLLOW ME, MY
FRIENDS. WE WILL GO TO MY HOME—WHERE I HAVE

THE WHEELS IN SAFE STORAGE—AND RECTIFY THIS
UNFORTUNATE SITUATION IMMEDIATELY."

"A free-range 'bot," Spuckler said to me as we
stepped back into the busy walkways of Omega
Doy Zarius to follow Thirgen. "You see more and
more of 'em these days: 'bots that ain't got no master 'cept themselves."

"You mean Thirgen lives alone?" I said. "Who
fixes him when he breaks down?"

"Free-range 'bots do their level best *not* to break
down," said Spuckler. "They practice somethin' called
rotational part replacement: they keep stockpiles of
spare parts and swap in fresh components whenever
they need 'em. Even *before* they need 'em." He paused
and added: "I reckon Thirgen's been pretty good at the
game. He's a third-generation Gax unit—you can bet
that's where he took the name Thirgen from—and
that's about as old as they come. Gax is tenth genera-
tion, and most folks think *that's* older than the hills."

We turned a corner and climbed a ramp leading
up to Thirgen's home: a small windowless structure

at the very top of a boarded-up warehouse. By now the sun had almost set, and the cool evening air made me eager to get inside.

"Check out Thirgen's wheels," said Spuckler as we neared the top of the ramp. "They're in real good shape."

They were indeed. Thirgen's wheels, as far as I could see, were the only parts of him that *didn't* need replacing.

"He must've been plannin' *years* in advance, buyin' Gax's wheels," said Spuckler. "Still, ya can't be too careful, I suppose."

Thirgen invited us in, apologizing for the lack of chairs (robots don't have a whole lot of use for chairs), and immediately rolled into a different room to get the wheels.

"I WON'T BE A MINUTE," he said. "MAKE YOUR-SELVES AT HOME."

A quick examination of the room offered ample proof that Thirgen not only practiced rotational part replacement: he was pretty much obsessed with it.

One whole wall was given over to helmets of various shapes and sizes. A smaller section was devoted to necks. Out of curiosity I pulled a drawer open and found dozens upon dozens of robotic eyes. "Man," I said. "This guy is stocked for the next century."

"THE NEXT *SEVERAL* CENTURIES, ACTUALLY," said a new and not very friendly voice. The voice belonged to Thirgen, who had now returned to the room.

His appearance had changed so much he was almost unrecognizable. The kindly-old-grandpa Thirgen had been nothing but a disguise. The battered, ratty exterior had shifted aside to reveal a shimmering armored surface beneath. His eyes were sharp, wide open, and darting back and forth with unnerving precision. The rattles and squeaks had utterly ceased, leaving nothing but a cool, steady hum: the high-tech buzz of cutting-edge hardware in top-notch condition.

And he was not holding Gax's wheels.

He was holding a laser pistol.

"CAN'T BE TOO CAREFUL."

Chapter 20

Spuckler threw Gax into my arms and leaped at Thirgen without a second's hesitation.

PYOOM! PYOO-PYOOM!

Three expertly fired laser blasts brought Spuckler crashing to the floor. He was injured—not critically, thank goodness, but enough to keep him from rising to his feet anytime soon.

Mr. Beeba put his hands up. Poog hovered silently in space. I dropped to my knees and huddled with Gax on the floor.

"I HAVE NO INTEREST IN INJURING HUMANS, TOOGOLIANS, OR"—Thirgen cast an eye at Mr. Beeba—"OR WHATEVER IT IS YOU ARE." Mr. Beeba simply stood there shaking, too frightened to be offended. "I HAVE NO DESIRE TO INJURE ANY*ONE* OR ANY*THING*. ALL I WANT . . ." He locked his mechanical eyes on Gax. ". . . IS YOUR ROBOT."

Thirgen rolled forward until he was within a foot of Gax and me.

"TO THINK I WAS HAPPY JUST TO HAVE ACQUIRED THE WHEELS. BUT YOU HAVE BROUGHT ME SOME-THING *FAR* MORE VALUABLE: A COMPLETE TENTH-GENERATION GAX UNIT. SO VERY HARD TO COME BY. WHY, I'LL BE SCAVENGING PARTS FROM HIM FOR MANY YEARS TO COME." Thirgen cocked his head to get a better look at Gax's neck. "ONCE I'VE DEACTI-VATED HIM, OF COURSE."

Thirgen raised his laser pistol and pointed it squarely at my nose. "EARTHIANS ARE KNOWN FOR BEING COMPLIANT AND MALLEABLE. I TRUST YOU WILL NOT PROVE TO BE AN EXCEPTION TO THE RULE."

"Y-you can't have him," I said, straining to lift Gax as I rose to my feet (with wheels or without, he was *very* heavy) and moved as far away from Thirgen as I could. "You don't even *need* him." I felt a cold, hard surface press into my back and realized I was up against one of the walls. "Look at this place. You've got a *mountain* of spare parts in here. More than you'll ever use."

"PLENTY OF NECKS AND BODIES AND WHEELS, YES," said Thirgen. "BUT HEADS . . ." He moved forward and the laser pistol closed to within an inch of my nostrils. "HEADS ARE *EXCEEDINGLY* RARE THESE DAYS. I'VE ONLY GOT TWO OF THEM AT THE MOMENT"—he gazed hungrily at Gax's head— "AND NEITHER OF THOSE HOLDS A CANDLE TO THIS ONE." He drew closer and examined Gax's head from several angles. "EXCEPTIONAL CONDITION. NO WONDER HOFFELHIFF REFUSED TO PART WITH IT."

"You don't scare me," I said (though he did, in the extreme). "If you want Gax, it'll be over my d-dead body."

"NO, MA'AM," said Gax, straightening his neck

like a man before a firing squad. "IT'S NOT WORTH IT. *I'M* NOT WORTH IT. HAND ME OVER TO HIM BEFORE SOMEONE GETS HURT."

I looked down at Gax and spoke to him as firmly as I could. "Gax, I don't ever want to hear you talk that way again. We're a *team*. And I'm not handing you over to anyone." I turned my gaze from Gax to Thirgen. "Least of all this twisted . . . greedy . . . *freak* of a robot."

"OVER YOUR DEAD BODY, EH?" said Thirgen, extending the laser pistol until its muzzle pressed into the flesh of my nose. "NOT MY FIRST CHOICE. BUT IF YOU INSIST . . ."

My heart was pounding like crazy. Sweat was pouring down my cheeks. I shot a glance at Poog, who was regarding me with a strangely calm expression. He opened his mouth and uttered two brief gurgly sentences.

"Poog is telling you to hand Gax over," said Mr. Beeba, his voice trembling. "He has a very clever plan for outsmarting our foe."

Poog gave Mr. Beeba a highly annoyed stare.

"Sorry," whispered Mr. Beeba. "Wasn't supposed to translate that last bit."

"YOU CAN HAVE ALL THE PLANS YOU LIKE," said Thirgen, "AS LONG AS YOU GIVE ME WHAT I WANT."

I took a deep breath and placed Gax's body in two of Thirgen's waiting arms.

"SPLENDID, SPLENDID," said Thirgen. "IT'S EVEN MORE IMPRESSIVE UP CLOSE." Thirgen casually raised a third mechanical arm—one with a tiny pair of wire cutters on the end—and inserted it into a spot beneath Gax's head. Without a second's hesitation, he snipped.

FZITCH

Gax's head flopped to one side. He shuddered for a second, then became as limp and lifeless as a stringless marionette.

"No!" I cried, tears stinging my eyes. I knew Gax was not deactivated for good. Still, it was like witnessing a murder.

"AH, BUT I MUST PROTECT THE CIRCUITS," said

Thirgen. "MUSTN'T HAVE THEM BURNING AWAY
INSIDE A ROBOT THAT IS GOING TO BE CANNIBAL-
IZED ANYWAY."

I shot a glance at Poog. What was his plan?

Poog stared at me with his big shiny eyes. His
gaze burned into me. It's hard to explain, but I felt
he was trying to . . . I don't know, *beam* a message to
me or something.

I stared right back at him, trying my best to deci-
pher what he was trying to get across to me.

Poog's lips were shut tight. But somewhere, deep
inside my brain, I began to hear a word. It was like
having someone whisper in my ear. But not my ear,
exactly. Like someone whispering into a *new* ear, an
ear in the center of my head, an ear I never knew
I had.

Move was the word I heard. *Move.*

I stared at Poog, amazed. Poog simply nodded.

Move? I thought. *Move where?*

Then I understood: Thirgen's laser pistol was
still trained on me. If Poog's plan was to succeed, my

nose needed to be somewhere other than directly in front of Thirgen's laser pistol.

"THE HEAD IS A BIT RUSTED OUT HERE ON ONE SIDE," continued Thirgen, fascinated with his new acquisition, "BUT THAT'S NOTHING A SOLDERING IRON AND A BIT OF EFFORT WON'T FIX."

I glanced at Poog. He nodded again, reassuring me that if I followed his instructions, everything would be okay.

"THIS MISSING SCREW IS GOING TO BE A PROBLEM, THOUGH," said Thirgen. "THEY STOPPED MANUFAC-TURING THESE *YEARS* AGO."

I drew my nose back from Thirgen's pistol. Sure enough, Thirgen was so entranced with his new pos-session he didn't even notice.

"STILL, THEY'LL BE ABLE TO MAKE A REASONABLE FACSIMILE OVER AT HAZZLE-SACK'S PLACE IF THE PRICE IS RIGHT. . . ."

I took a deep breath, bent my knees ever so slightly, and . . .

FSWIT

. . . dived to the floor.

PYOOM! PYA-PYOOM!

I heard the laser pistol fire but had no idea what it hit or how close it came to me. I rolled and turned just in time to see Poog rocket through the air and slam into Thirgen's body.

The two of them skidded across the room and crashed into a shelf full of mechanical arms.

KLANG! KLENG! TRUNG!

Dozens of robot parts came clattering to the floor as Poog and Thirgen rebounded and tumbled back into the middle of the room.

"FOOLISH TOOGOLIAN!" screeched Thirgen. "YOU'LL PAY FOR THAT WITH YOUR PURPLE HIDE!" One of Thirgen's mechanical arms punched a large red button on the floor, and immediately a series of armored walls shot down from above, sealing off all the robot parts from the escalating battle.

PYOOM! PYOOM! PYA-PYA-PYA-PYOOOM!

Mr. Beeba and I leaped behind a pillar as Thirgen began firing wildly around the room with his laser pistol. Poog dodged each blast perfectly. With each attempt to hit Poog, Thirgen left a new smoldering hole in the ceiling or floor. It soon became clear that Poog was purposely tricking Thirgen into using up his ammo and laying waste to his own home at the same time.

Finally Thirgen stopped firing and took stock of the situation. Poog hovered in space and issued a short gurgly statement.

Mr. Beeba, cowering with me behind the pillar, poked his head out to offer a translation. "P-Poog advises you to return our friend and his wheels before there is any further damage."

Thirgen was unimpressed. "I AM A FREE-RANGE ROBOT. I TAKE ORDERS FROM NO ONE. AND CERTAINLY NOT FROM THE LIKES OF YOU." He drew Gax even closer to his body and rolled back several yards, onto a ramp leading to an alcove near the ceiling. "NOW, IF YOU WILL EXCUSE ME"—he was already halfway up the ramp—"I WILL BE OFF TO PUT MY NEW ACQUISITION IN SAFEKEEPING."

Rather than follow Thirgen, Poog floated over to my side and spoke to me urgently in Toogolian.

"Poog wants you to climb on top of him," said Mr. Beeba. "Like you did back at Alia Rellapor's castle."

"You mean he's going to—"

"Quickly, Akiko!" Mr. Beeba pointed at Thirgen.

A section of the ceiling had moved away, leaving nothing above us but open air. "Thirgen's going to make good his escape! There's no time for questions!"

I did as I was told, allowing Poog to snuggle into my belly and lift me into the air. Looking up, I saw Thirgen, with Gax still locked firmly in his grasp, roll into a horseshoe-shaped contraption that had been designed to fit perfectly around his body. On either side of the thing was a variety of rocket boosters.

K'CHAK! K'CHAK!

As soon as the machinery was attached, it roared to life . . .

FFFRRRRAAAAWWWWWwwww

. . . and lifted Thirgen through the ceiling. He was now a combination robot–rocket ship and could fly anywhere he wished to go.

"Go, 'Kiko!" cried a hoarse voice from behind me. It was Spuckler, who had recovered just in time to give me the send-off I needed. "Show that sucker that Earthians ain't nothin' to be messed with!"

Chapter 21

The towering skyscrapers of Omega Doy Zarius rushed by on either side as Poog rocketed me through the air. The sun had now vanished into the Moonguzzit Sea, and a chill wind whistled through my hair and across my arms, giving me goose pimples. Busy neon-lit streets and sidewalks sailed past below. It was like being in an airplane, but with no seat, no window, and . . . no airplane. Once or twice we came frighteningly close to a fleet of passing hover taxis, but Poog was very much in control: I was never in any real danger of hitting anything as long as I held on to him with all my might. Which I did, of course, so tightly that he could probably barely breathe.

After a minute or two of speed that made my pigtails shoot back at a ninety-degree angle, Poog and I began to gain on Thirgen. For the time being, Thirgen was unaware that we were in pursuit, and closing in on him was a simple matter of staying on his trail and flying as fast as Poog could manage.

Gax was still firmly in Thirgen's clutches, but if I got close enough to grab hold of Gax, maybe . . . just maybe . . . I could begin to pry him free.

Soon we were within thirty feet of Thirgen and Gax.

Then twenty feet.

Then ten.

Then five.

I thrust one arm forward and watched as my outstretched fingers drew ever closer to Gax's body. The fires of Thirgen's rocket boosters were just a foot or two from my face, and the heat was almost unbearable. Still, if I could just deal with it and stay focused . . .

My fingers were now no more than a foot away from Gax's neck.

Now just six inches.

Now just three.

fsutch

I gritted my teeth in triumph as my fingers closed around Gax's neck and held fast.

Thirgen's head spun around and regarded me with both anger and astonishment.

"IMPOSSIBLE!"

He pushed a few buttons on the front of the rocket boosters and immediately began corkscrewing through the air in an effort to make me lose my grip.

I stretched my other hand out and snapped it around Gax's neck just as I began to whip around and around, whirling like a human propeller. At the same time, I realized with a sickening turn of my stomach that Poog was no longer anywhere near me. My hold on Gax was the only thing keeping me from plummeting to the bustling streets of Omega Doy Zarius, many hundreds of feet below.

"LET GO!" cried Thirgen.

He leveled off for a moment, pushed more buttons, then soared skyward. Within seconds we had blasted dozens of stories into the air and risen to such a height that my ears were popping like mad. By the time Thirgen eased off from his ascent, we were higher than the tallest skycraper in the city. I stared down at the seemingly microscopic streets below, horrified in my certainty of what was coming next.

Sure enough, Thirgen entered into a nosedive of cataclysmic proportions.

vvvvvvvvv

Forget roller coasters. Forget bungee jumping. Nothing could make me feel the sheer terror I experienced as we plunged straight down in an accelerated free fall . . .

vvvvvvvvvvvvvvvv

. . . toward what promised to be a spectacular crash somewhere on the pavement below.

No, I told myself. *Thirgen's crazy. But he's not suicidal.*

Down we went. Down, down, down . . .

And he's definitely not going to allow Gax to get dam-
aged. If I can get close to as much of Gax as possible . . .

Tensing the muscles of my arms, I began to pull myself along Gax's neck. I had to get as close to his body as I could before Thirgen got anywhere near the ground.

vvvvvvvvvvvVVVVV

We were now rocketing down through a narrow space left between two enormous skyscrapers. Windows sped past me on all sides as a crowded marketplace below grew nearer and nearer.

VVVVVVVVVVVVVVVVVV

Using all my strength, I grabbed hold of Gax's body and pulled myself against it. I was now wrapped around Gax like a coat, and Thirgen could do no damage to me without risking damage to Gax as well.

VVVVVVVVVVVVVVVVVVVVVV

My eyes grew wide with horror as the tents and crates and fruits and vegetables of the market-place rushed up to meet us. I pulled myself even

more tightly against Gax and half closed my
eyes as . . .

SHUP

SPOP

FLUP-FLUP-FLUP

. . . Thirgen made a hairpin turn and hurled
himself horizontally through the marketplace at
top speed . . .

FWAP

SKOP

SPLA-DAP-DAP-DAP-DAP

. . . smashing into tables, ripping through sheets
of canvas, sending terrified alien shoppers diving to
the ground in all directions.

SHUP

SHAP

SHEP

SHIRP

SP'SHHHHhhhhhhhhhhhhhhh

Finally we shot out of the marketplace, spiraling
wildly through several impossibly narrow alleyways

before Thirgen returned to a more or less even keel. Then he soared back up to the tops of the sky-scrapers and spun his head to see how much more punishment I could take.

What he saw couldn't have been very pretty. I was covered with a variety of splattered vegetables, bro-ken eggs, and several pages of the *Daily Skraboosh,* which were plastered to my body with a substance that had the consistency, flavor, and eye-stinging qualities of spicy mustard.

What he saw couldn't have been very reassuring, either: I was still holding on to Gax, and was not planning to let go anytime soon.

"ALL RIGHT, THEN," said Thirgen. "IT SEEMS YOU MUST BE DEALT WITH MORE DIRECTLY."

Thirgen rocketed from the city center and car-ried me all the way to an abandoned stretch of waterfront many miles out of town. The whole area was marshy and damp, and obscured by a heavy blanket of mist rolling in off the sea. Thirgen found a secluded port and glided down for a landing on one of its dilapidated piers. He then released Gax's lifeless body, and Gax and I thudded to the boards together.

"THERE WILL BE NO ONE TO INTERFERE WITH ME HERE," said Thirgen, as much to himself as to me.

I looked around. The last traces of twilight had left the sky, and only the glow of an orange moon allowed me to see the rotted-out hulks of engines surrounding us—the remains of some long-forgotten shipment, unloaded, unclaimed, and left there to rust in the elements.

There was a moment's pause; then . . .

K'CHIK-K'CHIK-K'CHIK

Three separate mechanical arms folded out from the right side of Thirgen's body, each of them holding a laser pistol. The weapons spun, rotated, and locked in on three different parts of my body: an arm, a leg, a foot.

K'CHIK-K'CHIK-K'CHIK

Three more arms with laser pistols emerged

from the left side of Thirgen's body, mirroring the actions of their counterparts on the right.

There would be no dodging Thirgen's lasers this time.

I was trapped.

Chapter 22

Thirgen didn't fire right away. He simply stood there, regarding me with cold indifference.

"YOU KNOW, GAX UNITS ARE PROGRAMMED NOT TO USE WEAPONRY AGAINST SENTIENT BEINGS," said Thirgen. "IT'S VERY DEEPLY INGRAINED IN OUR MOST VITAL CODES. THAT'S WHY YOUR PEG-LEGGED FRIEND ESCAPED WITH JUST A FEW INCAPACITATING WOUNDS: MY CODES PREVENTED ME FROM HITTING HIM WHERE I REALLY WANTED TO."

All was silent apart from the waters of the Moonguzzit Sea gently lapping against the pier. The ghostly moon, now more red than orange, hung low in the sky, blurred by the increasingly thick fog.

"THE LASER PISTOL I HAD AIMED AT YOU EARLIER WAS A BLUFF. I COULDN'T HAVE ACTUALLY FIRED A LASER BEAM INTO YOUR SKULL." Thirgen paused, then added, "NOT ON SUCH SHORT NOTICE, ANYWAY."

My heart, already pounding, began to thump even harder.

"YOU SEE, THE CODES CAN BE OVERRIDDEN."

ttzzz

One of Thirgen's laser pistols changed targets ever so slightly, from my left arm to my left shoulder.

"IT JUST TAKES A LITTLE EXTRA TIME, THAT'S ALL. I'M OVERRIDING THEM RIGHT NOW, EVEN AS I SPEAK TO YOU."

My head was spinning. I was shaking like mad. There had to be some way out of this.

"ANOTHER MINUTE AND I'LL BE FULLY CAPABLE OF FIRING THESE LASER PISTOLS WHEREVER I WISH," said Thirgen. "YOUR HEAD, LET'S SAY. OR YOUR HEART. OR BOTH, SIMULTANEOUSLY."

Sweat poured down my face.

chzzzz-ttzzzzz

Two more of Thirgen's laser pistols changed direction: one to point at a thigh, the other to point at my stomach.

"ANOTHER FORTY-THREE SECONDS, TO BE PRECISE."

I closed my eyes. A sickening feeling began to rise within me that after all this time, after all the scrapes I'd been through with Spuckler and Poog and Gax and Mr. Beeba, it was all going to come to an end right here.

No, I thought. *Poog is here somewhere. He wouldn't abandon me like this.*

There was a soft splashing noise somewhere behind me, as if a slightly larger wave had suddenly hit the pier. I felt water soak through my shirt and dampen my back.

"TWENTY-NINE SECONDS."

fftzzz-kkzzzz-mmzzz

Laser pistols were now pointed directly at my head, my neck, my heart—laser pistols that Thirgen would be fully capable of firing in less than half a minute.

Wait, I thought. *Water against my back: that's impossible. We're a good fifteen feet above the water.*

"SEVENTEEN SECONDS."

I reached behind my back, and my fingers touched something cold, wet, slimy, and *alive.* I instinctively pulled my hand away.

chzzz-vvzzz-ffzzz

Now all six laser pistols were aimed at either my head or my heart. There was no way any of them would miss at such close range.

The slimy thing behind me, I thought. *It's there for a reason.*

"NINE SECONDS."

I reached behind my back again and felt around for the creature I'd touched a moment before. As my fingers touched it, I heard the voice—Poog's voice—the voice that spoke to me in the ear within my ear, the ear in the very center of my head. . . .

The voice said: *Throw.*

"FIVE . . . FOUR . . . THREE . . ."

I closed my hand around the slimy thing and without even looking to see what it was threw it straight into an opening on the side of Thirgen's body.

FFFSSSSHHHHHHHhhhhhhhhhhhh

There was a hissing sound. Sparks began shooting out of Thirgen in all directions.

"TWO . . . ONE . . ."

I jumped and rolled to one side.

PYOOM-PY PYOOM-PYOOM!

The laser pistols fired erratically in all directions,

each missing me by a pretty wide margin. The slimy thing I'd thrown at Thirgen was causing him to have a major meltdown.

But then, how could it have caused anything less? The thing I'd thrown was a hurpleskap.

"I'LL . . . ," said Thirgen, his voice beginning to degenerate into electronic gibberish as a flurry of yellow sparks blew from the base of his head, *"GET*: : . : : : . : *YOOU*: : : . : : : . : : . : *FFOORR*. : : . : : : . . . . : : : : : . : : : . : : : *THIZZZZZZZZ."* His voice trailed off into a low-pitched mechanical gurgle, like a tape recorder struggling to play after its plug has been pulled.

All at once Thirgen's neck gave out, allowing his head to collapse into his body as if he were a child's toy. One last minor fizzle of sparks sprayed out of his body and . . .

chsssssssssshhhhhhhhhhhh

. . . he ceased moving altogether, instantly becoming just as broken-down—and utterly harmless—as the other pieces of machinery surrounding him.

I turned and stuck my head over the edge of the dock.

Sure enough, there was Poog, smiling up at me.

He'd been with me all along.

Chapter 23

"You made the hurpleskap jump out of the water, didn't you?" I said to Poog once my heartbeat had slowed back down to a reasonable pace.

Poog nodded.

"You were able to get him as high as the edge of the dock, but you needed me to throw him the rest of the way."

Poog nodded again.

I paused, smiled at Poog, then did my best to put on an extremely angry face as I shouted loudly enough to send my voice echoing crazily across the water. "Well, what *took* you so long, you little goof-ball!" Poog made a gurgly sound that may or may not have been Toogolian laughter. "I was *dyin'* up here!"

I wanted to ask him how he made me hear words in my head. How he had helped me discover an ear I never knew I had. But something told me those questions were best left unasked, that they were probably even unanswerable. For now, there was only one thing I needed to say to Poog. Something I knew I'd be saying to him again and again.

"Thank you, Poog." I took a deep breath, newly grateful for the simple ability to breathe. "Thank you."

Poog just smiled and blinked once or twice with his big shiny eyes.

"A toast to Akiko and Poog," said Mr. Beeba the next morning, standing up and raising a frosty mug of smagberry cider back at Chez Zoof. "I can think of no heroes more courageous, more selfless, more heedless of danger, more persevering in the face of adversity, more . . ."

Touched as I was by Mr. Beeba's effort to honor us, my mind drifted away from his onslaught of adjectives and turned instead to the events of the previous evening. Poog had left me on the pier and returned to find Spuckler and Mr. Beeba back at Thirgen's house. By then they had managed to find Gax's wheels (no small feat: Thirgen had amassed so many that it took deductive reasoning worthy of Sherlock Holmes to be sure they got the right set), and so the three of them returned to the fogglenaut and made their way to the pier to meet up with me and Gax. We all piled in and set sail for Gollarondo as Spuckler soldered on Gax's wheels and replaced the vital wire that Thirgen had clipped, instantly bringing Gax gloriously back to life.

We arrived in Gollarondo in the middle of the night and slept in the fogglenaut until morning. Since fogglenauts couldn't fly as Spuckler's ship did, we had to climb an incredibly long stairway to get up to Gollarondo. By the time we reached Chez Zoof, we were all almost ready to collapse from exhaustion. Thankfully, there was a huge table of delicious food waiting for us when we got there, courtesy of none other than Nugg von Hoffelhiff: he'd been following our exploits from afar, and wanted to congratulate us on our success. And that was just for starters. He'd also sent over a brand-new spaceship, identical to Spuckler's in every way, apart from the fact that it ran better, made less noise, and had not yet begun to rust. "Sissy car," said Spuckler, trying to conceal his delight.

". . . more fastidious in ferreting out the felonious falsities of a fearsome foe, more dogged in their determination to disrupt the deranged designs of a dastardly—"

"Hang on, hang on," I said, jumping to my feet and motioning Mr. Beeba back to his chair. "First things first. We've got to raise a glass to the guy who suffered more through all of this than any of us." I turned my eyes from Spuckler to Poog to Mr. Beeba, and, finally, to a certain newly reconstituted robot. "Gax."

"Hear, hear!" said Spuckler.

"Quite right," said Mr. Beeba, after recovering from the indignity of having his toast interrupted.

Gax raised his head as I cleared my throat.

"Here's to the best robot in the entire universe," I said. "May he never again fall to pieces, and may all who cross his path know as deeply and as truly as I do that he is more—*much* more—than the sum of his parts."

Robots don't shed tears, but Gax looked as if he were about to.

"To Gax!" bellowed Spuckler, splashing all of us with a fresh spray of smagberry cider.

"To Gax!" we all cheered.

Mr. Beeba then finished his toast—taking pity on us, he wrapped it up in a mere two and a half minutes—and we all dug in to what was probably the most scrumptious breakfast any of us had ever had. It started with freshly prepared jeelee eggs for everyone and went on and on for several hours, ending only when Spuckler dozed off, his head snuggled up against Gax.

Much as I didn't want to speak—or even *think*—about Thirgen ever again, I knew that we had a responsibility not to leave him there on the pier outside Omega Doy Zarius. I talked it over with Mr. Beeba and we agreed that he should be retrieved and given a thorough reprogramming so as not to go back to his violent ways. Mr. Beeba was sure there'd be no trouble arranging for a search warrant that would allow Thirgen's mountainous excess of necks, heads, bodies, and wheels to be seized and redistributed among robots that truly needed them.

The remainder of the day was devoted to rest, relaxation, and just generally kicking back and admiring the spectacular upside-down skyline of Gollarondo. All in all, no one had anything to complain about. Well, except Mr. Beeba, who discovered that the SMATDA had been shut down for emergency repairs when one of its floors collapsed into one of its ceilings. But just between you and me, the fact that the afternoon was going to be devoted to something other than ancient tomes and dusty artifacts only provided another reason to raise a glass of smagberry cider.

That night Spuckler, Gax, Poog, and Mr. Beeba flew me back to Earth. We arranged to meet the Akiko replacement robot out in the woods near my aunt Lucille's house around two in the morning. She arrived a little late, explaining that Cousin Earl had been up watching his collection of *America's Funniest Home Videos* tapes and that she'd had to wait for a moment of uproarious laughter to cover for the screechy-hinged door on the back porch.

"Just be glad you have robot skin and not real skin," I told her as she climbed into the ship along with the others. "The mosquitoes are murder out here tonight."

I gave everyone hugs and kisses goodbye and made Spuckler promise that no matter what happened, he would never again under any circumstances put a spaceship in Wacahoota Creek. He agreed but first made me admit that it was "pretty darned funny."

Gax was the last to board, and before he did, I gave him another little hug.

"Thanks, Gax," I said.

"BUT WHATEVER FOR, MA'AM?"

"For trying so hard to save me. You know, way back in Gollarondo, when I almost fell off the patio at Chez Zoof." I patted Gax on the helmet. "That one spontaneous act of bravery nearly cost you your . . . well, I don't know if *life* is the right word when it comes to robots."

I paused and searched for the proper thing to say. It didn't take me very long.

"Life *is* the right word when it comes to robots," I said. "Or when it comes to you, at least."

"THANK YOU, MA'AM."

"All right, now get on that ship," I said, "before I take you back to the house and make you watch TV with my cousin Earl."

Gax bounced happily on his springs and rolled up the ramp into the ship.

I stood there in the woods and watched the spaceship rise into the sky until it became indistinguishable from the stars surrounding it. Then I walked back to Aunt Lucille's place and, using the replacement robot's trick of sneaking in during one of Earl's guffaws, tiptoed back to the guest bedroom without anyone seeing. I was so tired I should have just gone straight to bed. Still, there was something I had to get started on. Something that couldn't wait.

I pulled a notebook out of my backpack, grabbed a pen, and sat up in bed with a bunch of pillows behind my back.

My name is Akiko, I wrote. *You know how whenever something really amazing happens to you, you just can't wait to tell all your friends about it?*

Read all of Akiko's adventures!

Akiko on the Planet Smoo

ISBN: 978-0-440-41648-7

Akiko in the Sprubly Islands

ISBN: 978-0-440-41651-7

Akiko and the Great Wall of Trudd

ISBN: 978-0-440-41654-8

Akiko in the Castle of Alia Rellapor

ISBN: 978-0-440-41657-9

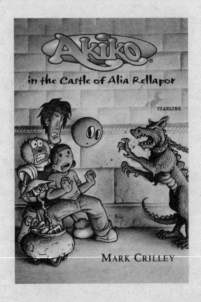

Дkiko and the Intergalactic Zoo

ISBN: 978-0-440-41891-7

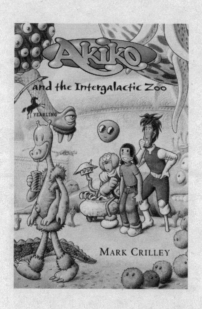

Akiko and the Alpha Centauri 5000

ISBN: 978-0-440-41892-4

Akiko and the Journey to Toog

ISBN: 978-0-385-73042-6 (hardcover)
ISBN: 978-0-440-41893-1 (paperback)

Akiko: The Training Master

ISBN: 978-0-385-73043-3 (hardcover)
ISBN: 978-0-440-41894-8 (paperback)